A CHECKUP FOR THE COWBOY

ELK MOUNTAIN RANCH BOOK TWO

RUTH PENDLETON

CONTENTS

CHAPTER 1

A bead of sweat trickled down Thomas Matthew's face as he stood at the far end of a field, debating his options. He needed to be on the other side of the fence if he wanted to finish his work for the day, but that meant crossing in front of the angry bull who was quite miffed at being woken up. The look in the bull's eyes meant business, and Thomas was quite sure he didn't want any part of that transaction.

Thomas usually took the long way around, but something at the end of the field had caught his eye. If he was seeing things right, one of the cows was laying at an awkward angle, with a hoof straight up in the air. That wasn't how cows slept, and it certainly wasn't how they relaxed. Something was wrong, and Thomas wasn't going to leave until he knew what it was.

He measured the distance in his mind. If he got a running head start, he might be able to beat the bull to the other side of the pasture. He gave it maybe a seventy percent chance that he wouldn't end up gouged by the sharp horns that sat on the bull's head. During their last encounter, the bull had won. Thomas wore the scar down his hip, a battle wound that ached whenever he stretched the wrong way.

Some days racing a bull to the fence seemed worth the chance, but Thomas wasn't sure this was one of them. If the cow was injured, she was going to need real help. Not a human who was potentially nursing a new wound of his own from the bull's horns. He went back to the ATV and drove it in a wide circle around the bull's enclosure, stopping a little ways back so he didn't startle the cow.

When he got off the ATV and walked closer, the problem became clear. A section of the four-pronged barbed wire fence had broken off. The missing wire was nowhere to be seen, but Thomas could piece together what happened. As he got closer to the cow, his suspicions were confirmed. She lay on the ground, her hoof stretched awkwardly in the air to avoid cutting it further on the wire that was wrapped around her legs.

"What mess did you get yourself into?" he asked. He spoke softly, trying to calm the terror in the cow's wide, brown eyes.

Further inspection of the wire showed that it was completely wrapped around her hindquarters. It looked like she had gotten spooked at some point and ran straight for the fence. In doing so, she tangled herself in the wire.

This wasn't going to be a one-person fix. Thomas pulled out his phone, debating which sibling to call. With the sun slanting towards the horizon, the odds of his brother Porter still being on the ranch were slim. Porter had been waking up an hour earlier each day to get through his work so he could spend time with his girlfriend Emily in the afternoons.

It was a toss-up between Reid or Bree. Reid was working in the hay fields at the opposite end of the ranch. Depending on where he was with the tractor, it could take a while for him to get over to Thomas.

Bree was the clear choice. Thomas listened to the phone ringing, crossing his fingers that she hadn't stayed after school to hang out with friends.

She answered on the fourth ring. "Hey, Thomas. What's up?"

"Hi, Bree. I need some help. Can you bring wire cutters to the south field? One of the cows got herself tangled up in the fence."

Thomas heard a chair scraping across the floor. "I'll be there in a minute."

With Bree on her way, there was nothing to do but wait. Thomas didn't want to leave the cow. Her hide already had lacerations from where the wire cut into her body. If he could keep her calm, hopefully she wouldn't cut herself any further. She was worn out from struggling, which meant she had probably been laying there for at least an hour or two.

The cow lay fairly still until the roar of the ATV startled her. Then she began to struggle. "Easy there, girl," Thomas said, but it was too late. The cow began to roll back and forth in the dirt, digging the wire deeper into her body.

Thomas flung his arms across her torso, pinning her to

the ground. "Help is almost here," he said. He gritted his teeth and dug the toe of his boots into the ground, trying to hold her still as the wire cut his shirt.

"Hurry up, Bree," he yelled. The cow was not happy to have a two-hundred-pound man pinning her down.

It took Bree just a few seconds to assess the situation when she got close. "Does it matter where I start?"

"Nope. We just need to get this wire off her before she cuts herself too deeply."

Thomas focused on the cow, trying to keep her still while Bree snipped at the wire. It felt like an eternity before she stepped back. "I think I got enough. You can let her go."

Thomas freed the cow's head, letting her stumble to her feet. She shook her head once and then made a beeline for the other side of the pasture, leaving the tangled wire behind.

"Thanks, Bree. I couldn't have done it without you."

"Poor cow. Do you think she'll be okay?"

"Probably. I'll keep an eye on her, but none of the cuts looked too deep."

"You could call Hazel." There was a glint in Bree's eye that was easy to interpret.

Thomas shook his head. "We don't need a vet until there is an actual problem."

"You could call her anyway." Bree tried to hide her smirk, but Thomas caught it.

He wasn't going to give his sister the satisfaction of knowing how badly he really did want to call Hazel. They were just friends though, and they would never be more. She had made that perfectly clear.

Thomas shook his head. "Sorry, Sis. No matchmaking for you today."

"Fine. Your loss." Bree pointed to Thomas's shirt, where his sleeve was torn from the elbow almost to his wrist. "That looks pretty bad. Are you okay?"

Thomas lifted his arm to check it. That's when he saw the long, shallow cut snaking across his skin. He had been so focused on the cow; he hadn't even noticed when it happened.

"I'll be fine. I didn't even notice I was bleeding." He glanced down at his dirt covered shirt and stained jeans. Being a rancher had a lot of perks, but the constant amount of laundry he had to do wasn't one of them. At least he wasn't going to have to worry about washing his shirt. It was heading straight for the trash.

Bree planted her hands on her hips. "What is mom going to say when she hears you've been wrestling cows? I don't think that's the smartest thing you've ever done."

Thomas reached out to tousle his youngest sister's hair. "How about we keep this little cow intervention between the two of us? I'll help you with your math homework tonight if you don't tell mom."

Bree grinned. "The math this year is going to do me in. I keep reminding myself I only have to make it through two more years of high school. Then I can go to college with Finn and Wyatt."

"Yeah. I'm sure the twins will make it a fun freshman year."

"Assuming Wyatt hasn't done anything to drive his professors too crazy."

Thomas grinned. His nineteen-year-old brothers were known for their mischievous side, but they always meant well. He missed having their energy around the ranch.

"I'm going to get some new wire to patch the fence. Then I'll be in for dinner."

Bree pointed to his arm, where blood was beginning to seep through the shirt sleeve. "You may want to take care of that before mom sees you."

"Good call. Thanks again for your help."

Thomas walked to his ATV and sat down. The adrenaline from tackling the cow was wearing off, and his arm was beginning to throb. He watched Bree crest the hill and disappear down the other side. Then he pulled up his sleeve to examine the cut up close.

He wasn't going to need stitches, but the barbs had been rusty. He was going to have to watch it to make sure it didn't get infected.

Thomas wasn't sure where to rank the cut on his list of injuries. He was used to getting scratched, kicked, and bitten. Through the years he had accumulated his fair share of scars. It came with the territory. Thirty years on the ranch had taught him that nails were sharp, hooves could kick, and even a chicken could play dirty if you were trying to steal her eggs. This cut didn't come close to his top ten for injuries, although the shirt was a goner.

He pulled the ripped sleeve back down and headed for the barn to gather a new coil of wire and some screws. It didn't take long to fix the fence, but his arm was throbbing something fierce by the time he headed back to the house.

Walking inside, Thomas's nose was bombarded with the scent of herbs. Mom Matthews may have been a regular rancher's wife, but she cooked like she was head chef of a five-star restaurant. It smelled like she had been grilling, the heady aroma of herbs and spices mingling with the woodsy scent of smoke. Thomas held a hand over his rumbling stomach, more than ready to dive into the food.

A quick glance at his arm reminded him of his compromised state. He kicked off his boots by the door and hung his hat on the hook.

"Dinner is almost ready," his mom called.

"Great, because I'm starving." Thomas poked his head into the kitchen so he could talk to his mom. "I've got to shower real quick. Then I'll be down to help."

"Thanks, Thomas." Mom Matthews turned her back on him when the oven timer went off. He hurried past the kitchen door and headed up the stairs.

Bree was coming out of his room when he reached the hallway. "How's the arm?"

"I'll live."

She smacked his shoulder. "I'm serious. I put a roll of gauze and some ointment on your bed in case you need to wrap it. Mom didn't see me sneaking them out of the first aid kit."

Thomas reached out to hug his sister, but she squirmed away. "I can tell you've been wrestling cows today. I could smell you when you walked in the door."

"That bad?" He wasn't surprised.

Bree's grimace turned into a smile. "Okay. You might not smell quite that bad, but a shower won't hurt."

"I'll be quick." Thomas turned towards his bedroom, a smile on his face. He hadn't been sure what to think about having a baby sister born when he was in junior high. At the time, she seemed like a nuisance; a fussy baby that was constantly under foot and into trouble. They hadn't really been close until his dad died. Then the dynamics shifted. Bree went from being the tag-along little sister to someone who needed a father figure to look up to.

In a matter of days, the oldest Matthews brothers had banded together. They were going to take care of their baby sister no matter what it took. Sometimes it was difficult to tell who spoiled Bree the most between Porter, Reid and Thomas.

He pulled clothes out of the closet and then grabbed the gauze. The cut had stopped bleeding, but it was safer to wrap it than let an infection set in. The wire certainly wasn't the cleanest thing on the ranch, but it wasn't the worst. Either way, he wasn't taking chances.

Thomas felt like a new man when he stepped out of the bathroom. He loved being able to wash the grime of the day down the drain. That was when he let all his frustrations of the day go as well. It helped him to lock a smile on his face when he went down to eat. He wanted to be pleasant no matter what was happening in his personal life.

He took a few minutes to slather ointment on his long, jagged cut. Once it was wrapped with the gauze, Thomas knew he was going to have to be extra careful if he wanted to avoid his mom's eye. She had a sixth sense when it came to helping her children. Chances were, if she didn't know about his injury by the end of dinner, she'd know by the end of the night.

It wasn't that he was embarrassed that he'd gotten cut. He had been ready to help the cow with whatever means it took. He couldn't feel bad about that. The problem was adding one more burden to his mom's impossibly heavy plate. She was working hard to keep the ranch afloat. The brothers were carrying a bulk of the heavy lifting, but Mom Matthews kept the family in order. She didn't need to be bothered with a simple injury that would heal in a matter of days.

Thomas walked into the kitchen, salivating at the sight of the T-bone steaks stacked on a platter. "What can I help with?" A timer began to ding as if it had been waiting for Thomas to come in.

"Will you grab the scalloped potatoes out of the oven?" Mom asked.

"I'm on it." Thomas reached for a pair of oversized oven mitts, slipping them on his hands. He pulled a heavy pan out of the oven, wincing as the movement pulled against his cut.

The eagle eyes of his mom followed his every move. "Did you burn yourself?" she asked.

"Nope. I'm good." Thomas slid the potatoes to the counter. He was going to have to practice his poker face a bit more. She studied him for a moment longer and then handed him a bowl of salad.

"Okay. Well, that's the last of the meal. Will you help me carry the food to the table?"

Thomas reached for the platter of steaks, balancing them on one arm while he held the salad with the other. He left the potatoes on the stove for his mom to grab and headed to the table. Once the food was set, he rang the dinner bell. Within minutes, the siblings were crowding around the table.

The dining room was filled with chatter. Thomas listened to the various conversations around him, finding comfort in being surrounded by the people he loved best. Emily had come with Porter, which wasn't surprising. She fit in with the family like she belonged there.

Thomas had watched his brother bury a wife eight years previously. When she died, Thomas realized just how fragile relationships could be. His dad died not long afterwards, cementing in Thomas's mind that relationships led to heartache. He was content being a bachelor, until Porter began dating Emily.

Watching how his brother was able to open his heart again after a tragedy gave Thomas hope. Emily was perfect for Porter. Seeing the two of them together brought a pang to Thomas's heart. He wanted a relationship like Porter had, but there was only one woman he was interested in. He had known her for years but that didn't help.

Hazel would never agree to go out with him.

CHAPTER 2

$\mathcal{H}$azel's hands were covered in soap. She had been rubbing them together for the past minute, working up a lather to wash away the lingering smell of latex from her skin. As a vet, she was pulling gloves off and on all day, changing them out between patients. That meant that although her hands were clean, they picked up a strong smell by the end of the afternoon.

The ritual of that final scrub signified the end of the work day, which Hazel desperately needed. It was only Wednesday, but the week had started with a constant pull from one emergency to the next. She was exhausted. As Hazel dried her hands on a faded blue towel, she prayed that she'd actually be able to enjoy the rest of the night with no interruptions.

Calving season in the fall in a small ranching town meant that there were often late-night calls. Most of the ranchers knew the basics for a safe delivery, but Hazel was the one they called when things got complicated. She'd followed in her dad's footsteps since she was old enough to walk, stepping in to take over his veterinary clinic when his health began to fail. As his right-hand woman, she had helped deliver more animals than she could count, but each delivery brought an adrenaline rush. She never knew which ones would go sideways. Losing animals was the most devastating part of her job.

Hazel slipped into yoga pants, the soft cotton a direct contrast to the stiff jeans and boots she wore during the day. Yoga pants were another signal to her body that it was time to relax. Armed with a good book and a mug of warm milk, Hazel made her way to her bedroom. She propped her pillows against the headboard and opened the book, letting her imagination get swept away by the story. The hero was leaning in for a kiss when her phone began to ring.

The noise shattered the peace of her evening. It was a shrill, demanding tone that sent an immediate wave of exhaustion through her body. The call was from the clinic's after-hours receptionist. The fact that Jana was interrupting Hazel during her off-hours meant there was an emergency somewhere that only Hazel could handle.

Hazel inhaled for a count of three and let the air flow from her body as she blew away the frustration of her disrupted evening. She picked up the phone with a cheerful hello, masking the anxiety that the call brought her.

"I'm sorry to bug you," Jana said, "but it's the Stringham ranch. Labor stalled for one of their cows and she needs help. Mr. Stringham is worried about her."

Hazel eyed the half-empty mug sitting on the night-stand. It was time to swap out the relaxing milk for a cup of coffee with enough of a kick to wake her up. "Tell them I'll be there in twenty minutes."

She stood in the bathroom, debating briefly about which clothes to wear. The delivery was sure to be messy, so she grabbed the pair of jeans she had shrugged off what felt like moments before, looking at her yoga pants with longing as they slipped to the floor. She couldn't wait to put them on again.

Hazel was out the door with a few minutes to spare. By the time she got to the Stringham farm, the sky was streaked with pink and orange clouds, and she had settled into vet mode. The yoga pants and good book were forgotten as she turned her focus towards the task at hand.

John Stringham came running to meet her when her truck pulled in. Those sorts of greetings always made her feel like a celebrity. Unfortunately, her job was much more difficult than waving hi to adoring fans. She grabbed a large duffle bag out of the back of her truck and followed a frantic Mr. Stringham through the barn until they came to the stall where the cow was laboring.

A ten-second assessment of the situation set Hazel into overdrive. She needed to get the calf out immediately, or they'd risk losing both the mother and the baby. Mr. Stringham and his sons jumped to attention as Hazel began calling out orders. As the men rushed around her to help, a wave of calm settled over Hazel. This was the moment when the world stilled. All that mattered was getting the baby safely delivered so it could take its first breath.

The delivery was over in minutes. Thankfully she had been able to free the hooves so the mom could deliver naturally without needing a c-section. Hazel stood back and watched the mom as she began to clean her calf. His spotted coat stood out against the pale straw from the stall.

Mr. Stringham ran a hand through his hair. "I don't know how you do it, but you're a lifesaver."

"I'm glad I was able to help." Hazel began to gather her tools while keeping an eye on Mr. Stringham. Most of the owners she worked with were the same. They got so worked up about their animal's health, that when the adrenaline from the job wore off, they became shaky themselves. She usually encouraged the ranchers to sit for a few minutes before getting back to work.

"Mom and baby are both going to be fine," she said. "I'll swing by in the morning to make sure she still looks good, but you're out of the danger zone. I'd recommend getting a good night's sleep so you can help her in the morning."

"I hear you. I'm going to keep watching until the baby is up on his feet. Then I'll call it a night."

Hazel held back her knowing grin. Mr. Stringham was going to stay up for hours watching the mom and baby. At least he had six sons who could help share the load when he needed to sleep in. She knew better than to argue with the stubborn nature of a worried rancher.

The final rays of sun were piercing the sky when Hazel made her way down the hill, Old Ranch Road dimly lit in the dusk. She glanced towards the Matthews ranch, where a certain cowboy was most likely kicking off his boots and getting ready for bed if he wasn't already asleep.

Thomas's rugged face danced through her mind. Girls swooned when he walked by, yet he seemed oblivious to his effect on the women around him. His stern eyes narrowed when they worked out a problem, but they turned to liquid chocolate when they looked at Hazel. His dark hair looked incredibly soft, but Hazel wasn't going to run her hands through it to check. He tried to be clean-shaven, but by the late afternoon a five o'clock shadow highlighted his rugged jawline.

They had been friends for so long, she could barely remember the time before they met. She had watched him grow up, but as he did, he began to carry the weight of the world on his shoulders. It was hard to watch her carefree, happy friend as his eyes lost their sparkle. The world hadn't been kind to the Matthews family, but Thomas somehow bore the brunt of that weight.

Hazel was so deep in thought, she didn't see the dog that darted across her path until it was too late. She slammed on her brakes, the truck skidding to a stop with a small thump. The sound sent a chill down Hazel's spine. How could the town vet, of all people, be so careless as to hit a dog?

When she got out, the dog was nowhere to be seen. It didn't make sense. If she had hit the animal, he would be lying on the ground somewhere nearby. Hazel walked back to her cab to turn the high beams on. Then she grabbed a headlamp from the glove box and slid it onto her forehead.

If there was a hurt animal out there, she was going to find him.

A quick look around the truck didn't reveal the dog. Hazel walked down the road a few yards, calling for him. She stopped occasionally, listening for any whimpering sounds, but the night was quiet. Hazel's heartbeat sped up. When an animal was injured, time was of the essence. She circled back to her truck, her eyes darting from side to side.

She was so intent on her search, she didn't notice the shadowy figure walking towards her truck until he spoke.

"Everything okay?" he asked.

The deep, rumbling bass was familiar, but that didn't stop Hazel's heart from leaping out of her chest. She jumped, letting out a small scream. "Thomas. You scared me. What are you doing here?"

Thomas stepped back from the truck into the circle of light from her headlamp. "I was going to ask you the same thing. I could see your truck's lights from my porch. When they stopped moving, I figured something was wrong."

Hazel's heart slowed to a steadier beat for about half a second. Then she realized Thomas was going to want an answer for why she was sitting there. She could feel the knots in her stomach tying into a ball. What if his dog was the one who had run in front of her truck?

She held her stomach, fighting the urge to throw up. "I think I hit a dog."

Thomas's dark eyebrows creased; the worry lines too deep for a man who had just turned thirty. "You did?"

"Yeah. He darted right out in front of me, and I didn't

stop in time." The reminder of what had been distracting Hazel was standing in front of her, looking at her with his mesmerizing eyes. She couldn't tell Thomas she had been thinking about him when the dog ran into the road. That would add all sorts of embarrassment to the situation.

Thomas reached for Hazel's arm. He pulled her close, wrapping her in a friendly hug. "Where is the dog now?"

Hazel leaned against Thomas's side. She had been hugging Thomas for years, from a quick congratulatory hug when they graduated from junior high to a comforting hug when she broke up with her first boyfriend. The hug meant security, friendship, and trust, but never anything romantic. A hug between friends was all it was, so why was Hazel's body aching for more? She allowed herself a second to enjoy the way she felt, leaning against Thomas's side. Then she pushed back.

"That's the problem. I can't find it."

Thomas raised an eyebrow. "You hit a dog, but you can't find it now? How did you manage that?"

Hazel put her hands on her hips. She'd love to have a battle of wits against him, but there was an injured animal out there. It wasn't time to banter. "I slammed on my brakes, and there was a thump. I just didn't see where the dog went."

Thomas rocked back on his heels to study Hazel. She wanted to slink down into the cab of her truck; anything to get away from the scrutiny of his watchful eyes.

"Are you sure you hit it?" he asked.

Hazel opened her mouth to retort, but then she closed

it. She hadn't actually seen the dog getting hit. It was the sound of the truck that threw her off.

"I thought I did. There was a definite thump when I slammed on my brakes."

Thomas leaned against the side of the truck. "What did the dog look like? Small and wispy? Large and menacing? Maybe it was a ghost."

Hazel couldn't relax. "It was definitely a real dog. He was black, probably a lab, but it happened so fast, I didn't get a good look. He could be a mix."

Thomas nodded. He lifted his thumb and forefinger to his lips and let out a loud whistle. "Scully. Come here, boy," he called.

Hope rushed through Hazel's body, giving her temporary relief from the fear that was making it difficult to breathe. If Thomas was calling the dog, they'd be able to find him. As embarrassing as it was to have hit an animal, at least Hazel would be able to treat his injuries.

The whistle echoed through the night air, waiting for Scully to answer. Hazel was beginning to give up hope when a deep bark answered the call. Her heart lifted. If Scully was barking back, he couldn't be hurt too badly.

Thomas whistled once more, and before long, a shadowy figure came bounding up to them.

"Is this the guy you hit?" Thomas asked.

Hazel squatted down by the dog's side and brushed her hands over Scully's body, feeling for any bumps. She watched him to see if any of the spots she pressed on were tender, but all Scully did was wriggle closer so he could lick her face.

"I don't understand," she said. "He seems perfectly fine, but I could have sworn I hit him."

Thomas knelt by Hazel, joining her in petting the very happy dog. "He looks great to me."

Scully responded by jumping up and running off to chase whatever creature he presumably had been chasing before he was interrupted.

Hazel shook her head. "It felt so real," she whispered. She was relieved that Scully was fine, but totally confused about the thump she had felt.

Thomas turned on his phone's flashlight and angled it under the truck. "I think I found your animal."

The words sent a wave of dread through her body. Hazel had been looking for the wrong creature. "Oh no. Is it bad?" Visions of a poor animal stuck under her tire flashed through her mind. How had she missed looking there first?

Thomas began to laugh. "Apart from the six-thousand-pound truck smashing it, I'd say it's going to be just fine." He pointed under the tire.

Hazel held her breath as she leaned forward to look. Then she began to laugh. "I can't believe I got so worked up over hitting a rock."

Thomas reached for her body, pulling her close to his chest. "That's what I love about you. You have the biggest heart of anyone I know." He released her and stepped back. "Are you good here?"

Hazel nodded. "I think so. Thanks for your help."

Thomas headed back to the ranch, but the pressure of his arms around Hazel's body lingered.

It wasn't the first time Thomas had said he loved her. Hazel wished it meant more to him than a casual saying between friends.

"I love you, too," she whispered. She let the wind carry the words away where no one could hear them. It didn't matter if she loved Thomas Matthews. He was her friend, and that was going to have to be good enough.

CHAPTER 3

Reid was waiting to pounce when Thomas came back to the house.

"So, what was the problem out there? Someone get a flat tire or something?"

Thomas smiled. "It was Hazel. She thought she hit Scully, but she didn't. She accidentally hit a rock."

Reid's brow furrowed. "What about Hazel? Did she get hurt?"

Thomas kicked off his boots and headed for the family room, plopping down on the couch. "She was shaken up, but she seemed fine when I left her."

Reid sat at the other end of the couch. "Are you ever going to ask her out?" He was blunt as usual, but Thomas was used to it.

It was a valid question. "Here's the thing. I never wanted to date anyone unless they were a good friend first, right?"

"Yeah." Reid nodded. "I remember you saying that."

"Well, I tried that friends first, date later thing with Lisa. And we all know how that turned out."

Reid ran a hand through his hair. "Yeah. That was hard to watch. You were crazy about her."

"Exactly. I mean, I know I'm the one who eventually called things off, but she still avoids me. It's been over ten years and the woman can't even say hi." Thomas drummed his fingers on the edge of the couch. "I saw Lisa at the grocery store last week and she turned and ran so fast, you'd think she saw a bear. She hates me that much."

Reid fake yawned to hide a smile.

"Hey." Thomas punched his brother's shoulder. "It's not funny."

"You're right. I'm sorry." Reid straightened his shirt. "The thing is, Hazel isn't like Lisa. Just because things didn't work out with one woman doesn't mean that every other relationship is doomed. Hazel isn't the type of person to shut someone out."

"I didn't think Lisa was, either, but here we are. Hazel chose to stick with me after my breakup with Lisa. I'm not going to jeopardize that friendship."

"Man. Why are relationships so complicated?" Reid asked.

"I don't know, but that's why I don't want to ask Hazel out. If she ended up like Lisa, I'd be losing so much more than a girlfriend. I'd lose one of my closest friends."

Sitting in the family room wasn't helping Thomas's nerves. He walked to the kitchen and pulled the freezer open. "Hey Reid," he called. "Do you want any ice cream?"

"You know it," Reid said. "I'll be there in a few."

Mom Matthews kept a well-stocked freezer. Thomas pulled out containers of mint chocolate chip and caramel swirl ice cream. He was reaching for the bowls when Porter came into the room.

"Ice cream time?" Porter asked. "I'm in."

Thomas pulled out an extra couple of bowls with a knowing smile. It wouldn't be long before Bree and their mom came to the kitchen, too. Thomas needed to ask his brother a question before everyone else joined them.

"Hey Port?"

Porter looked up from the drawer where he was grabbing spoons. "Yeah?"

The question he wanted to ask died on Thomas's lips. "How are things going with Emily?" he asked instead.

Porter slid a stack of spoons across the counter. "It's way better than I could have dreamed. She makes me happy."

"Aren't you afraid of getting hurt?" That was the question Thomas really wanted to know. How was his brother so willing to date when he knew that marriages could end badly?

Usually, Thomas was the one with the answers. He had tried to figure out things on his own when Porter had been caught up in the grief of losing his first wife. Now Porter seemed to be moving forward with his life while Thomas was stuck with fears of the past looming over his shoulder.

Porter folded his arms on the counter and studied Thomas's face. Thomas knew that look. His brother was trying to figure out why Thomas was asking the question.

"I guess the short answer is that I decided that being

alone is difficult and being in a relationship is difficult. I had to figure out which one meant more to me, since there are no guarantees in life. When I met Emily, I knew I'd rather risk heartache and give our relationship a try than be alone for the rest of my life."

"But what if it doesn't work out? Wouldn't a friendship with her be better?"

Porter took the container of mint chocolate chip ice cream from Thomas. "Is this about Hazel?"

As usual, his brother was spot on. Thomas took a bite of ice cream to delay his answer. "I love having her as a friend. She's one of my closest friends, but what if there's more to our story? What if she's the person I'm meant to spend the rest of my life with?"

The thought of starting a relationship with Hazel sent a pang of longing through Thomas's body. Was there a future where he could tell her he loved her romantically and not just as a friend?

Porter held his spoon in the air. "You asked if a friendship with Emily would be better. While I can't imagine my life without her, I also know a friendship would never be enough. When I'm with her, I can't keep her out of my arms. I wouldn't want to be friends if it meant standing to the side and watching her fall in love with someone else."

"But if things go wrong, you could lose her entirely."

Porter nodded. "That's a risk I'm willing to take. I haven't been friends with Emily for years like you've been with Hazel. That might have changed things."

"So, it makes sense to keep our friendship where it is." Thomas trusted Porter's advice.

"I didn't say that. The way I see it, you guys already have a lot of great communication skills. Why not give it a try?"

Thomas was starting to answer when Bree walked in. "What are you going to try?"

"Nothing," Thomas said.

"Asking Hazel out," Porter said, sidestepping to avoid Thomas's lunge towards him.

Bree looked back and forth between her brothers. "I'm going to believe Porter's answer on this one. When are you going to ask her out?"

Thomas lifted his ice cream bowl, looking for a quick way to escape but it was cut off when Reid entered the room.

"Thanks for getting everything out," he said. "Can you pass the caramel swirl?"

As Porter slid the ice cream to Reid, Thomas steadied his hands against the counter. He had one chance to change the subject away from his dating woes before the casual conversation with Porter turned into an inquisition.

"Did you hear that Hazel is due any day?"

Porter raised his eyebrows while Reid began to laugh.

"*Hazel* is due?" Bree asked. "I can tell who is on your mind."

Belatedly, Thomas realized his mistake. "I meant Hannah. Our horse Hannah is due any day."

It was too late. The siblings were circling and there wasn't anything Thomas could do to stop them.

* * *

As he had expected, the ice cream party had turned into a full discussion on the pros and cons of Thomas asking Hazel out. He knew where his heart stood, but he was terrified of messing things up.

Standing in a stall filled with dirty straw didn't help calm his mind. Each scrape of the shovel against the floor sent a wave of questions through his body. Would Hazel say yes? Was she interested in someone else? What if they hit it off? What if he kissed her? The questions swirled through his mind.

What if they started dating and Hazel realized that she really didn't want to be with him? Or what if he didn't want to be with her? What if they really were better as friends? Each question was a string, tying his stomach completely in knots. The alternative of not asking Hazel out felt worse though.

She wasn't going to stay single forever. What if someone else caught her eye? The idea of Hazel seriously dating anyone else made him want to throw his shovel at the wall. Thomas was stubborn and opinionated, but he wasn't a coward. There was only one way to solve the Hazel question. That meant pulling up his bootstraps and using his words.

The county fair was only a week away. Apart from hosting the best selection of pies Thomas had ever tasted, the fair was also a perfect place to take Hazel. She loved flowers, and the county fair hosted one of the best shows in the state. Rumor had it, this year all the flowers were arranged to look like jungle animals.

They had been going together with a group for years to check out the flower displays. Maybe this year they could make it an official date.

Thomas's muscles were screaming for a break before he pulled out his phone. Hazel answered on the final ring.

"Hey Thomas," she said, her voice instantly calming the raging storm in Thomas's body.

"Hi Hazel. I was wondering if you'd be interested in going to the county fair with me next week." He gulped as he forced out the next words. "As a date."

His question was met with silence. Thomas kept talking. "I have tickets to the tractor pull and I hear Farmer Stringham is bringing some of his famous popcorn balls." The silence stretched on. "Or we could do the rides if you want. I know you like rollercoasters."

She still didn't say anything. Thomas smacked his hand to his forehead. All he'd done was ramble on and on when Hazel was clearly not interested.

After another excruciatingly long pause, Thomas held his phone away from his ear. Not only did Hazel not want to go on a date with him, but she had actually hung up the phone. The fact that she'd hang up on him rather than answer his question sent a pang to his heart.

So much for following the advice of his siblings to ask her out. He had already blown it.

Thomas got back to work, moving from one section of the floor to the next like the barn was going to explode if he didn't get the floors clean. His muscles were on fire, matching the discomfort in his stomach. He couldn't believe he had gone against his instincts and asked Hazel out.

The floor still had a fine layer of dirt on it, but it was clean enough. At least the stalls were clear and ready for the next time they had to lay straw down. With calving season in full swing, who knew when the next calf would be born? Thomas may have messed up his relationship with Hazel, but he wasn't going to mess up his responsibilities to the ranch.

The afternoon sun continued to dip lower in the sky, but Thomas wasn't ready to head inside. He had a storm raging inside his body that was there because his brothers had opened their mouths. If he went to the farmhouse and Emily was there with Porter, he would say something rude he didn't mean.

It was better for Thomas to stay outside. He swung open the large barn doors that housed most of the farm equipment. Surely there was some sort of a job he could do that would keep his hands busy. His eyes scanned the various pieces of equipment.

Back towards the far corner of the building was his dad's tractor. The old tractor had seen a number of good days before finally sputtering to a halt. Thomas had sat on his dad's lap as a young boy while he drove the tractor across the fields, pulling different pieces of equipment. Some of his favorite memories included his dad teaching him how to plow.

"Careful, son. Look behind us. What kind of lines are you making?"

Thomas had scrunched up his eyes. "Wiggles?"

Dad Matthews ruffled his hair. "Yes, son. Wiggly lines. And what kind of lines make our crops the happiest?"

"Straight ones!"

His dad had put a hand over Thomas's, helping to hold the wheel. Then he pointed to a post at the far end of the field. "Do you see that post over there?"

"The green guard?"

Dad Matthews had laughed. "I guess you can call it that. When we plow this field, we want to head straight for the green guard at the end of the field. He has magic powers."

Thomas could feel the excitement mounting. "What can he do?"

Dad Matthews helped Thomas to hold the wheel straight. "Count to ten." They moved forward at a steady pace as Thomas counted out loud. When he reached ten, he looked up at his dad. "What's the magic?"

His dad ruffled his hair again. "Look behind us. What kind of lines are we making now?"

Even years later, Thomas could remember the feeling of awe when he realized they were making straight lines. It felt like magic at the time. Now Thomas realized that the plowing post, like so many other things on the ranch, had a purpose. The post was there to guide the eye so he could stay on a straight path.

If only his dad was still around. He'd be able to help Thomas know what to do with his heart. His dad wasn't there but working on the tractor for a few hours would help him feel closer to him.

Thomas was sliding out from beneath the tractor when

his phone began to ring. He wiped the grease off his hands and looked at the caller ID.

Hazel.

He was tempted to let it go to voicemail. She had rejected him earlier after all. He wasn't sure how much more his heart could take. But even as he thought about ignoring her, his hand was reaching for the phone. It was Hazel. He would always answer.

"Hi Thomas," she said, her voice completely oblivious to the pain she had caused him.

"What's up?" Thomas asked. He was determined to keep things light.

"I'm sorry about earlier. I was heading through the mountains and my phone cut you off. You were saying something about the fair?"

Thomas jumped to his feet and began to pace. She hadn't heard him ask her out, which meant he had another chance. Was he brave enough to take it?

CHAPTER 4

*H*azel prided herself on being an honest
woman. She had built up a relationship with
her clients by giving accurate diagnoses, with all the available treatment options instead of the ones that would make her the most money. Sometimes that meant waiting to see if the animal got better on their own instead of prescribing expensive medications or recommending surgery.

With her deep sense of honesty, she couldn't shake the fact that she was lying to Thomas. The part about driving through the mountains had been true. So was the part about her phone cutting off.

The part she was leaving out was that she had distinctly heard what sounded a lot like her friend asking her out on a date. Dates were something people did when they were interested in each other. They weren't something Hazel and Thomas did together.

She hadn't actually heard the last word of his sentence,

but she had heard enough to leave her heart fluttering when the phone had cut out. The Mendon family lived far enough in the mountains that she knew she'd be out of cell range for a while to come. Her stomach had danced while she treated their dog Rufus, who had swallowed a large pinecone.

Now she was out of the mountains and on the phone again, waiting for Thomas to say the same words. If he asked her out for the second time, she'd know he was for real. And if he was serious about a date? Well, she didn't know what to think about that. Her heart jumped at the thought, but her mind was shouting at her to be careful.

"Yeah," Thomas said. "I was wondering if you'd like to go to the fair with me. He paused. "With a group. I was thinking we could go with Porter and Emily, and maybe a few other friends. Bree has been bugging me to take her to the fair ever since she heard about the miniature horses that are going to be there."

As Thomas prattled on, the hope in Hazel's heart slipped away. She had obviously misunderstood the part where he asked her to go to the fair with him. It wasn't a surprise that he was wanting it to be with a group. Her imagination must have invented the date part.

"I'll have to see how my schedule goes." That was a safe answer. A large group of friends meant that Hazel's presence wouldn't be missed if she decided she wanted to stay home. She tamped down the surge of disappointment that flooded her body. There was a reason why people struggled to break out of the friend zone in relationships.

Hazel hung up with Thomas after setting a tentative

time for them to get together. Then she cranked her music up so she could sing her frustrations away. A few songs from the 90's were enough to get her blood pumping and her toes tapping. She was able to push the thoughts of Thomas away and sing instead of crying.

The music was a perfect distraction until a song came on that made Hazel pull her car to the side of the road, pounding her fist against the steering wheel with frustration.

As a senior in high school, Hazel watched her friend Lisa fall in love with Thomas. She listened to Lisa while she gushed about their first date. Lisa couldn't wait to go to prom with him.

The evening of prom, all the girls gathered at Hazel's house to get ready. The smell of hair spray followed behind the girls when they walked down the stairs, where they gathered in the front room in a sea of satin and taffeta dresses.

There was a collective squeal when the doorbell rang. The girls quickly stood, brushing their hands down their dresses to smooth any lingering wrinkles. When the boys arrived, they filed in one by one, reaching for their date's hands to slip on a floral corsage. Hazel watched the door, but her date never came.

Thomas was the first to notice Hazel standing in the corner, trying to discreetly wipe the tears from her eyes. He assessed the situation, leaned over to whisper to Lisa, and together they marched to Hazel's side, wrapping her in a hug.

"It's settled," Lisa said. She took off her corsage and slid it onto Hazel's wrist. "You're our date."

No one at the dance could see how Hazel's heart was breaking that night. Everyone assumed her tears had to do with being stood up, but really it was the heartbreak of watching Thomas dancing with Lisa all night. Prom was nearing the end when Thomas broke away from Lisa and walked to Hazel's side.

"I'm not your proper date, but every girl deserves a dance on prom night. Can I have this dance?"

He swept her into his arms, his strong muscles defined even back then. As they danced across the floor, Thomas sang the words softly to Hazel, changing the lyrics just slightly so they melted her heart. "I'll be the greatest love of your life." By the time the song was finished, she was his completely, but he hadn't meant the words for her.

Ten minutes later, Thomas was dipping Lisa back and sharing their first kiss in front of a gymnasium filled with students while Hazel's heart broke completely.

She thought she had removed that traitorous song from her playlist, which was why she was caught off guard, crying on the side of the road.

"Get it together, woman," she scolded herself. She needed a distraction immediately before she began to wallow in self-pity.

The Lord must have been watching out for her because a few minutes later, her best friend called.

Loud music thumped in the background, the beat making it difficult for Hazel to hear the voice on the other line.

"Can you hear me?" Steph yelled.

"Steph? Are you there?" Hazel asked. "I can barely hear you over the music.

"Yeah. Hold on a sec."

The phone was muted as the music disappeared abruptly and then Steph was back. "Sorry. I didn't realize how loud it was over here."

"Where are you? It sounds like you're having a party."

Steph laughed. "Kind of. I'm at the Spotted Cow Diner. They have the coolest band here tonight. Do you want to come?"

Hazel glanced in the mirror at her puffy eyes. The diner was far enough away, the swelling would be gone by the time she got there. It was just the distraction she needed. "I'm on my way."

When she got to the diner, Steph was waiting outside with a group of friends. "Millie is the one that dragged us here, but I'm not sure who likes the band best between me and Dawn."

"Why am I not surprised?" Hazel asked. "So, who is playing tonight?"

"They're called the Talking Cats, which is kind of a ridiculous name, but it fits them," Millie said.

"They're actually really good though," Steph said. "That's why we called."

Hazel released her hair from her ponytail and shook it, letting the blond waves fall around her shoulders. "Let's do this."

She was met with the smell of barbeque chicken when she went inside. The smell permeated the restaurant which was filled to capacity. Every table was full, with a few extra chairs surrounding the makeshift stage that stood in the center of the room.

The band played upbeat songs; the kind that made people want to dance. Sure enough, before long, the front tables were cleared down and rolled to the side of the room to clear the way for a small dancing area. Hazel loved that part of living in a small town. The owner of the diner loved inviting local talent to perform, often turning dinner service into an impromptu concert.

Oftentimes the people on the stage surprised Hazel. She would treat a rancher's horse in the morning only to see that same rancher belting out a song in the spotlight that night. The group currently playing had some new faces.

Hazel leaned close to Steph. "Who's on the keyboard?"

Steph grabbed her hands with a loud squeal. "He's cute, right?"

A few people turned in their seats to see what the commotion was, but thankfully the band launched into a long guitar solo, pulling the attention away from Steph's outburst.

"Are you trying to embarrass me in front of the entire town, or just half of it?" Hazel asked, gritting her teeth.

"Don't worry," Dawn said. "If you listen to the buzz around us, you'll hear that most of it is about the keyboard player. I wonder where he's from."

"There's one way to find out." Before Hazel could stop her, Millie was holding two fingers to her mouth and whistling loud enough to be heard above the cheering crowd. The lead singer grabbed his microphone. It took a second for Hazel to recognize him as Jonah Jack, a guy who dropped out of school their senior year to pursue a career in music. Somehow, despite all the bets against him, he was making it work.

"It sounds like we have a question," Jonah said, his eyes raking the crowd.

Millie waved her hand high in the air while Hazel stepped back, trying to blend into the crowd. She loved the exuberance of her friend, but not when it meant that all the eyes in the room were turning towards them.

"When are you going to introduce yourself?" Millie shouted.

Jonah grinned, showing his dimples. "It's probably a good time to do that," he said. "Trust the schoolteacher to be the one to call me out on bad manners," he said to the crowd. He winked at Millie, blowing a kiss her way.

Millie laughed good naturedly. "I've learned a few things teaching high schoolers," she whispered to her friends.

Jonah gestured towards a man wearing a dark t-shirt, his blonde hair slicked back to reveal a small earring in his ear. "On guitar, this evening, we have Max. Say hello to the crowd."

On cue, Max ran his fingers up the neck of the guitar, playing a complicated string of notes before finishing with a small bow. "Hi folks. It's good to be here in this guy's hometown. I'm sure you've got stories to tell us about Jonah later, right?"

The crowd chuckled and Jonah pointed to the drummer

who towered above the drum sets, the drumsticks dwarfed in his hands. "Sam is on the drums. What have you got for us tonight?"

Sam pounded out a quick rhythm which got the crowd cheering. His size didn't slow down the movements as he twirled his drumsticks in the air.

"Our keyboard master this evening is Stuart."

Stuart didn't wait for the rest of his introduction. He played a trill down the keyboard, his fingers flying down the keys. Somehow, even with his brown hair flopping over his eyes, he didn't miss a beat. At the end of his song, he looked over towards the women in the corner.

"So that's his name," Dawn whispered. "He really is pretty cute."

Hazel shushed her friend as Jonah scanned the crowd. "I'm Jonah, and together, we're the Talking Cats."

With the introductions out of the way, the Cats launched into a new song.

Hazel turned to Millie. "I can't believe you did that," she said.

"Hey. Now we know that the cute one is Stuart," Millie said.

Dawn sighed. "Honestly, they're all pretty cute. Even Jonah."

It was typical of her friend to see the good in everyone. Hazel reached for the women's hands, pulling them towards the center of the room. "Did we come here to look for men or did we come here to dance?"

"Both?" Steph asked.

Hazel shook her head. She already had a guy she was

interested in. As the music surrounded her, she let herself sink into the feeling of the moment. She was going to dance away all her frustrations about Thomas not being available. And then she was going to dance until her legs were so exhausted, she'd collapse into bed.

Hazel slipped her phone out of her pocket and switched it completely off. If there was a real emergency somewhere, they would have to call the vet in the next town over. Hazel was out of business for the night.

The Talking Cats played a few more songs, each one the medicine Hazel needed to take her mind off her worries. When they stopped playing, she came back to reality. "I need a drink," she said.

She led her friends over to the bar, ordering a glass of Coke. "Sodas are on me," she said. She was handing her card to the cashier when a deep voice spoke up behind her.

"You buying for the band tonight, too?"

Hazel spun around, coming face to face with Stuart. Up close, he was taller than she expected. He had mesmerizing blue eyes.

"What did you say?" Hazel asked.

"I was asking if you were going to buy our drinks." He smiled, his eyes dancing with amusement.

The cashier handed Hazel back her card. "You're going to have to be faster next time, Piano man."

Stuart's face fell with mock sadness. "Maybe next time," he said.

As the women stepped to the side, Hazel noticed that the band members were all drinking variations of soda. Then she remembered the Spotted Cow's rule. They didn't serve alcohol in their restaurant, and you weren't allowed to bring it in on concert nights. It kept the fighting down to a minimum, according to the owner.

It meant that you could get the best soda combinations at the diner. When Hazel was in a splurging mood, she would order her Coke with coconut and lime.

She followed after Steph, lost in thought, while her friend wove through the crowd. They found a table in the back and crowded in towards one side, making room for another group to join them. On concert night, there was no spreading out.

A few minutes later, a figure towered over them, blocking the light. "Are these seats taken?"

Hazel recognized Sam from the band. She turned to look at Dawn, her eye's wide, as the members of the Talking Cat band crowded next to him.

"So, we meet again," Stuart said. He slid into the booth next to Hazel, and for the first time in her life, she was at a complete loss for words.

CHAPTER 5

$\mathcal{H}$azel wasn't sure what she was expecting from the evening but sitting at a table with four men from the band hadn't even crossed her mind as a possibility. The fact that all the women knew Jonah made the evening feel comfortable. It wasn't long before everyone was joking together, telling the bandmates stories from high school.

"Do you remember when Jonah stole the classroom snake?" Dawn asked. She held a hand over her mouth while she laughed.

"Oh my gosh. I had forgotten about that," Millie said.

Sam raised his eyebrows. "Obviously we need this story."

"It was our sophomore year," Hazel began. "Mr. Higgins thought we needed to learn responsibility, so every week he'd assign a different pair of students to watch over his pet snake."

"When it was Jonah's turn," Millie chimed in, "the snake

went missing." Her eyes were welling up with tears from laughing so hard.

"The look on Mr. Higgins' face when he discovered that his snake was missing was priceless." Hazel took a sip of her soda. "He accused Jonah of being lazy and leaving the cage cover open."

Jonah shrugged and held out his hands. "How was it my fault that the snake escaped? I was just a high school kid trying to make it to graduation."

Steph slugged him on the shoulder. "That's what we all thought, until I went to your house the following weekend. Do you want to tell the band what I found?"

"Please tell me it wasn't the snake," Stuart said, shaking his head back and forth.

Millie held her stomach. "It was. That became one of our jokes the rest of the year. Somehow, a skinny, freckle-faced kid had outwitted the teacher and found himself a new pet."

"I couldn't help it. Mr. Higgins was keeping him in a cage that was way too small. When I lost my own snake, the opportunity to steal his was too tempting."

Hazel leaned back in the seat, her heart lifting with the laughter surrounding her. She was tired of overthinking things and worrying about what to do with Thomas. That was why, moments later, when Stuart leaned back to sit shoulder to shoulder with her, she didn't move. There was no rule that said she couldn't talk to the piano man.

Sam looked at his watch and cleared his throat. "As much fun as it is hanging out with you ladies, we've got another set to play."

"Will you guys be around at the end of it?" Jonah asked. He was leaning towards Steph, who hung on his every word.

"Maybe," she said, batting her eyelashes at him.

Hazel watched the exchange, crossing her fingers under the table. Steph deserved to be with a guy who would treat her well. Jonah, for all the guff they gave him, was still a great guy.

Stuart leaned close; his ice blue eyes freezing Hazel in place. "What about you? Is it okay if I see you again?"

It was an interesting idea. She bit the side of her cheek. "Maybe."

Stuart pulled out a napkin and scrawled his number across the top of it. "I'm putting the ball in your court. Call me."

The looks on her friend's faces were priceless. As soon as the men headed back to the stage, the women pounced.

"He gave you his number?" Dawn asked.

"Are you going to call him?" Steph added.

Hazel fiddled with the edge of the napkin. She pulled out her phone to put his number in, just in case, before remembering that her phone was turned off.

"I don't know, guys. I mean, he seems nice enough, but . . ."

She watched Stuart sit at the keyboard. He certainly fit the stereotype for guys she was interested in. Tall, handsome, with eyes that looked straight through her soul. She could easily get lost in that sea of blue. But even as she studied him, a different pair of eyes flashed through her mind.

Thomas was tall and handsome, too. He wasn't a mystery to Hazel. Standing next to Thomas felt as natural as breathing, except that Hazel was trying to change the game. She was letting her feelings get in the way of a friendship.

"You know what?" Hazel said, making an impromptu decision. "I'm going to give him a call tomorrow." She sipped her Coke while the friends around her talked over each other in their excitement. It was time to get out in the dating world and see if she could forget about Thomas.

It took Hazel three days to get the courage to call Stuart. Her final client of the day had been a small dog who had gotten into an argument with a porcupine. The dog had been trying to protect her puppies, but she got injured in the process.

Hazel admired the way Mimi's owner had handled things. She had gently wrapped Mimi in a towel and carried her in, having her son drive her to the doctor. As soon as Hazel gave word that all the quills were out, the woman gave her son a giant hug. Then she picked up the phone and called her family, assuring them that everything would be okay.

Watching the mom interact with her son left Hazel with a hollow feeling. More and more often, Hazel longed for someone to talk to at the end of the day. She could call her friends or family, but it wasn't the same as curling up on the couch next to someone she loved.

That is why she pulled out her phone, pacing back and forth while it rang. She almost hung up when Stuart answered.

"Hi Stuart. This is Hazel. From the diner where you guys played on Saturday." Each sentence took all her courage to say.

"It's only been a few days. There's no way I'd forget you that quickly. What's up?" He sounded smooth, like he was used to women calling him out of the blue. Hazel wasn't used to being around men who were so self-assured.

Hazel gulped. "Were you serious about going out some time?"

"I was. Does this mean you're asking me out?" The teasing lilt to his voice put Hazel at ease until she realized that she hadn't thought about any plans. Then she realized she had the perfect place to take him.

"How do you feel about county fairs?"

Stuart began to laugh. "Did Jonah tell you about my prize-winning guinea pig?"

"No. I didn't even know that was a category. I'm pretty sure I need that story now." Hazel pushed a few files to the side so she could lean against the counter. Talking to Stuart sent flutters through her body. Was she actually flirting? It had been so long, Hazel wasn't sure if she remembered how to do it anymore.

"In my defense, I was ten. At the time, I thought I was going to be a famous rancher. My parents turned down every pet request I could think of, in part because my first requests included a bull, a horse, and a pig. I kept asking for smaller and smaller animals until we landed on guinea pigs."

"That's not a bad place to stop. You could have ended up with a mouse or a slug."

Stuart's low chuckle sent another flutter through Hazel's stomach. His easy-going demeanor was putting her at ease.

"True. There's not much more to tell. I spent my days trying to teach the guinea pig tricks. It wasn't a fan of sitting on command, but it would come bop me on the hand if I held out a bit of lettuce. I knew that if I showed people, they'd be super impressed."

"And so you entered the guinea pig in the fair." Hazel could imagine how excited a young Stuart would have been.

"Yeah. As it turns out, there wasn't a category for guinea pigs. I was devastated."

"Didn't you say you won the prize?" Hazel picked up a pen and began to doodle on the side of one of her intake forms.

"Yeah." Stuart's voice got soft. "My cousin Nathan was showing a bull at the fair that year. He won first place, but as soon as he heard about how disappointed I was, he gave his ribbon to me."

"That is so sweet."

Stuart cleared his throat. "The crazy thing is that I didn't even know what he did. I genuinely thought my guinea pig had won a prize, and I told everyone I could about it. It wasn't until years later that I learned what Nathan had done. By then, I had already given up my ranching dreams and was starting my music studies. It's a good thing, or my heart would have been broken."

Hazel was doodling flowers across the top of the page. "Well, I can't promise you guinea pig contests, but our fair usually has some fun things to do. What do you think? Do you want to go?"

In the back of her mind, she could feel the warning bells going off. Thomas had asked her to the fair and now she was asking someone else. That could be troublesome. Then again, Thomas had said it was a group thing, which would make inviting Stuart perfectly acceptable. It was time to stop over analyzing her every single move.

THE DAY OF THE FAIR, the weather was perfect. A light cloud cover hinted at rain, but the day wasn't too hot. That would usually be great for a visit to the fair, but Hazel's stomach sank when she went outside. Bad weather would have given her an excuse to end her date early.

Hazel carefully curled her hair, pulling up one side in a small metal clip that Thomas had given her for her birthday years ago. Her hair hung down over her shoulder just the way he liked it. She didn't make the connection that subconsciously she was trying to look good for Thomas until she pulled on the blue V-neck that Thomas said made her eyes pop.

That wasn't going to do. She was going out with the group, but Stuart was her focus for the day. Not her friend.

Reluctantly, Hazel changed into a shirt that Thomas hadn't commented on, even though her eyes sparkled a little less.

Thomas had organized the group, so Hazel had no idea how many people were coming. All she knew was that she had to be at the ticket booth at ten am.

Somehow, in setting up the details with Thomas, she neglected to tell him that Stuart was coming as her date. She could barely explain to herself why she needed to bring Stuart, so how would she explain that to Thomas? It wasn't like he was going to care anyway.

Stuart arrived on her doorstep five minutes early. He looked handsome, with ripped jeans, a pair of designer shoes, and a button-down shirt that hinted at lean muscles underneath. He was going to stand out at the county fair full of ranchers, but that was kind of exciting to Hazel. She was ready for a break from normal.

Hazel's phone began to ring when she was climbing into the car. "What's up, Thomas?" she asked, glancing Stuart's way.

"Did you leave yet?" His voice had a sense of urgency that sent Hazel's stomach plummeting to the ground. She knew that voice. It meant that one of the animals was hurt.

"We . . . I'm just getting in the car now. Is everything okay?"

Thomas hesitated. "It's Bree. She started coughing about an hour ago and it keeps getting worse." The worry in his voice made sense. Thomas was always extremely protective of Bree.

Hazel's shoulders relaxed. A sick human was a lot easier to diagnose because they could tell you what was hurting.

"How serious is she? Do you need to take her to the doctor?"

"Nah. It's probably just a cold."

If he wasn't worried about Bree, then what was the urgency for? His tone didn't match the situation.

"Your voice made it sound like someone was dying. Is there anything else going on?"

Thomas cleared his throat. "Well, some of the other friends fell through, so it looks like it is going to be you and me with Porter and Emily. Is that going to be okay?"

Hazel's stomach began to free fall, sinking deep into the earth. Molten lava poured through her veins.

"That will be fine." Hazel reached for the button to hang up the phone, but she decided to come clean at the last second. "Oh. And Thomas?"

"Yeah, Hazel?"

"I'm bringing a date."

CHAPTER 6

Thomas couldn't believe what he was hearing. It sounded a lot like Hazel said she was bringing a date to the fair. To their date. He lowered the phone, staring into the distance as he tried to rearrange her words in his mind. How could she have a date? It didn't make any sense.

Porter waved his hand in front of Thomas's face. "Are you in there, brother?"

"It's Hazel." He looked at his brother, his eyes wide. What was he supposed to do now that she was bringing someone else?

"Is she okay?" Emily asked. The concern in her voice was real.

"I don't know. I mean, she must be, but she said she's bringing a date."

Porter placed a bag of snacks in the trunk. "Why would she bring a date when you asked her to go with you?"

Thomas dug a small divot in the dirt with the toe of his book. "Um. Maybe because I didn't actually ask her to be my date?"

Porter's eyes narrowed. "You're kidding, right? I thought the entire purpose of going to the fair was so you could decide how you felt about Hazel. Now you're telling us that you didn't even ask her?"

"Hey. I asked her to go. I just said it would be a group thing."

Emily shook her head. "You men. Why is it so hard to say what you want? I think you and Hazel would be perfect together."

"I agree with Emily. So, what do you want to do?" Porter asked.

Thomas gave the dirt a final kick and then shrugged. "I mean, I guess we still have to go. It would be rude to stand her up, even if she is with another guy."

He climbed into the back of the car, his stomach churning so hard, he was tempted to stay home like Bree. He hadn't messed anything up this badly since he hit a skunk crossing the road. Somehow, he knew this situation was going to stink worse.

Hazel was waiting near the turnstile when they arrived. She was talking to a short, slightly balding man. He didn't look like he had the strength to throw a pile of grass around, much less a bale of hay. Thomas tried not to be petty, but this guy was his competition. Based on height alone, Thomas was clearly winning.

Hazel threw her head back to laugh, and Thomas

couldn't get out of the car fast enough. No one should be making her laugh like that. Not even men who were clearly not her type. That was his job. He was halfway across the street when Hazel turned her attention to the man standing on the other side of her.

The man was tall and well-dressed. He looked like he could hold his own in a fight. If Hazel had a type of guy she was interested in, this guy fit the bill much better.

Thomas hadn't even given him a second glance when they had first driven by. He had been too busy scoping out the guy he thought was Hazel's date. She lifted her hand and brushed something off the second man's shirt, and Thomas froze in the middle of the street.

A horn blared, snapping him out of his thoughts. "Sorry," he mouthed to the driver. He was stepping up on the sidewalk when Porter grabbed the side of his shirt, pulling him to a stop.

"Are you sure you can handle this?" he asked.

"Her date is actually kind of cute," Emily added. Then she turned to Porter. "But not nearly as handsome as your brother, here."

Thomas groaned. "I can't believe I'm going to be spending the afternoon playing fifth wheel between you guys and Hazel and her perfect date."

"Sorry, bro. We'll be rooting for you." Porter released Thomas's shirt and moved to his side.

The last few steps to get to Hazel were torture. She was so engaged in her conversation with her date, she barely noticed when Thomas walked up.

"Hi, Hazel," Thomas said. He held his hand out to the man standing next to Hazel. "I'm Thomas. And you are?"

"Stuart." The man's handshake was firm, and he met Thomas's eye. As much as Thomas hated seeing Hazel with anyone else, at least the guy didn't seem to be a total jerk.

Hazel turned their attention to the balding man on the other side of them. "This is our new friend Casey. He was telling us all about the back entrance to the festival of flowers. From what he says, you can walk by all the stations where they assembled the displays."

Stuart held his arm out and Hazel grabbed it. "We thought after we got our tickets we'd head there."

"Do you think they will be prettier than the tulips?" Emily asked. She leaned against Porter's side and looked up at his face, sharing an inside joke.

The jealousy that surged through Thomas was difficult for him to tamp down, but he grinned. "If Casey says there is a back entrance, I say we go find it."

He turned towards the ticket booth, buying his ticket for just one. As he paid, he realized the entire afternoon was going to be much cheaper than he imagined. He had envisioned buying Hazel everything she wanted. If he had to spend $50 at a stupid ring toss booth so he could get her a giant stuffed toy, he was prepared to do so. Now it looked like Stuart was going to take his place.

Thomas was at a disadvantage, but he knew a few things about Hazel that Stuart didn't. Thomas pushed his way through the turnstile, a plan forming in his mind. If all went well, by the end of the day Stuart would be nothing more than a blip on the radar. He'd be someone they'd forget before the week was over.

The first step in Thomas's plan was a simple one. He was going to walk in front of the group so Hazel would always be able to see him. If Stuart was going to be by her side, then Thomas would always be in her line of sight. She wouldn't be able to forget him so easily.

He nodded as Hazel rattled off the directions to the back way. Then he took the lead, weaving his way through the crowd with occasional glances behind him to see if the group was coming.

On one of his turns, he forgot to watch where he was stepping. His boot came down with a squelch, and the smell that wafted up to Thomas confirmed his worst nightmare.

He was trying to scrape the horse manure off his boot when a clown pushing a wheelbarrow jogged up beside him. "Sorry, sir. I wasn't fast enough."

"It's no problem," Thomas said, gritting his teeth. He was beginning to regret his motto to keep his cool. Especially when Stuart doubled over with laughter.

"Oh man. That stinks. Get it? Stinks?"

It was worse when Hazel joined in, forcing a fake laugh at Stuart's lame attempt at a joke.

The clown gave Thomas directions to the closest water spigot so he could wash the sole of his boot clean. Stuart was still laughing as the clown walked away.

"I'm not sure if we can hang out with you today. You might scare everyone away with that smell." Stuart wrinkled his nose. "Seriously though, will a water spigot actually get those things clean?"

"I'm guessing you're a city boy," Thomas said. "My boots can take it." He glanced down at Stuart's shoes. They looked like the kind you'd buy online for hundreds of dollars. Thomas personally didn't get the appeal. If he couldn't wear the shoes on the ranch, why bother?

Stuart winked at Hazel. "This lady here knows where I'm from. The city bit doesn't bother her. Did she ever tell you where we met?" He draped an arm across Hazel's shoulder, which caused her smile to waver. She stepped slightly to the side, away from Stuart's advance, and hope bloomed in Thomas's chest. Maybe Hazel wasn't quite as enamored with Stuart as Thomas imagined her to be.

"I'm sure it's a fascinating story, but I've got a mess to take care of." Thomas excused himself from the group, his fists not relaxing until he was scraping the muck off the bottom of his boot.

So far, the day was shaping up to be a colossal failure. Not only was he flying solo, but the woman of his dreams was walking around with a city slicker who probably couldn't tell a horse from a cow. Thoughts of excusing himself early ran through his mind. He glanced at his watch. In the first ten minutes of coming to the fair, he had already managed to make a mess.

Thomas shut off the water spigot and headed to the sink so he could properly wash his hands. He was watching the bubbles swirl down the drain when he remembered the first part of his plan. He had to remind Hazel that he knew her best. The horse manure had distracted him, but he wasn't out.

The smell of cinnamon twists caught Thomas's attention. He crossed his fingers, hoping the right food vendor was there. The small cart was tucked between a food stand selling barbeque ribs and a balloon stand. Thomas ordered a Bun Bun Twist covered with cinnamon, caramel, and nuts. It combined the best parts of a cinnamon roll and a pretzel.

The first time they had gone to the fair together, Thomas and Hazel had shared a twist. He remembered trying to push her hair out of her face when it got stuck to her cheek. All he succeeded in doing was smearing more frosting down her face. Now it was tradition to always order a twist.

The crowd had gotten even larger when Thomas finally spotted Porter. He made his way through a herd of laughing teens and went to Hazel, holding the cinnamon twist out in front of him.

"Look what I found on my way back," he said.

Hazel's gasp of excitement was worth the hassle of having to clean up his boots.

"It's a Bun Bun Twist!" she said. She pinched a piece of dough between her hands, pulling the warm twist apart, but then, instead of turning to Thomas, she turned to Stuart.

"You've got to try this," she said.

Thomas watched as Hazel fed a bite to her date, his fists curling up by his side once again. For someone who was supposed to be reminding Hazel of their past, he wasn't doing a very good job. The way he saw it, the score was now Stuart - two, Thomas - zero.

Emily tapped his arm, leaning in close. "We still have all afternoon," she whispered. "Give her time to realize where her heart lies."

Hazel looked up from the gooey mess on the plate. "What are you two whispering about over there?"

Thomas gave Emily's arm a grateful squeeze. "Nothing much. We're just discussing how excited Emily is to taste the Bun Bun."

He stepped back as Hazel shared the plate around. If Emily was right, and it took Hazel all afternoon to get tired of her date, Thomas was going to have to toughen up.

"Anyone ready for the flowers?" he asked.

"Me," Hazel said.

Thomas walked towards the back entrance, this time keeping his eyes firmly facing forward. He was going to watch where he was going so they could get to the main attraction without another incident.

After a few minutes of walking, Thomas spotted the striped awning that Casey had told them about. When they got closer, he found a problem. He pointed to the large sign hanging on the door. **No Entry without a pass.**

"Your friend Casey forgot to mention the sign," Thomas said.

Stuart grinned. "No he didn't." He glanced at his watch. "Any minute now."

"What are we waiting for?" Thomas asked. "We should go around to the front."

"No need," Hazel said. She pointed to Casey who was rounding the corner with a large ring of keys in his hand.

"Are you guys ready for the behind the scenes tour?" Casey asked.

"Yes, please," Emily said.

Casey flipped through the keys, settling on one that looked pretty much the same as the other keys. He swung the door open and led the way through, into a dark hallway.

"Are you sure we're allowed to be here?" Thomas asked.

Hazel grinned. "Casey volunteers here. He is also one of the designers. I think he's being modest about the work he's done for the fair."

Casey blushed to the tips of his ears. "I tried my best," he said. "There were a lot of really impressive artists this year." He pushed through another door which opened into a large gymnasium filled with chicken wire, wood, flower petals, and green foam. Tables lined the walls, scattered with a various assortment of tools.

"This is where the florists assembled their designs," Casey said.

"Chicken wire was part of this?" Stuart asked. "Isn't that just for coops?"

Casey laughed. "If we've done our job right, you won't be able to see it."

Thomas was trying to think of something witty to say when he saw Hazel separate from the group and walk to a table. She rested her hand on the top before bending down to pick up a white rose laying in a sea of red petals.

In a blink of the eye, Thomas was transported back to the day of her brother's funeral. The memory of Hazel setting a single white rose on the casket before it was lowered to the ground was seared into his memory. Over the next few months, Hazel began seeing white roses everywhere she went. Whenever she found one in an unusual place, she called it a hug from Danny.

He walked to Hazel's side and wrapped his arm around her, not caring about the fact that she was there with another man. "Tell Danny hello from me," he whispered.

Hazel wiped a tear from her eye and nodded up at him. She was breathtakingly beautiful when she was vulnerable. Thomas pushed a strand of hair out of her eyes, tucking it behind her ear.

"Is everything okay here?" Stuart asked, breaking the moment as he stepped up beside them.

"Yep. I just got something in my eye," Hazel said. She turned to follow Stuart, giving Thomas's hand a grateful squeeze before she left.

As they followed Casey to the entrance doors, Thomas had hope. If Hazel wasn't willing to open up to Stuart, maybe there was a chance for him after all. He just had to figure out how to ditch the dead weight so they could get back to the double date the fair was supposed to be.

The main room held a display of incredibly complex floral arrangements, including a life-sized tiger. Hazel and Emily squealed with delight as they ran from one creation to the next, coming to an abrupt stop when they came to the water feature. A large salmon jumped out of the water while a mechanical bear paw tried to grab it.

The paw slapped down, splashing drops of water on the group. As it did, Stuart jumped back. "Hey. There should be a warning with this display. Not everyone wants to get wet."

Thomas had been expecting the entire day to be miserable but watching Stuart's reaction gave him an idea. He knew one activity he was pretty sure the city boy would hate. With any luck, Stuart would be gone before the hour was through.

CHAPTER 7

Thomas kept the conversation light while he walked through the rest of the flower displays. He oohed and ahhed with the rest of the group when they saw Casey's display. Casey had put together a large tree, with a blue and green striped snake uncoiling beneath the leaves. Compared to some of the show stopping pieces, it was easy to overlook the smaller entries.

Casey's display wasn't as large as some of the others, but Thomas was genuinely impressed. "I don't know how you put this together, man. I think my display would be a pretty vase that I asked my mom to help me arrange."

"It didn't win anything," Casey said, "but there were some tough competitors this year."

A flash of blue caught Thomas's eye. "Are you sure about that?"

He moved a branch of flowers to the side, revealing an honorable mention ribbon.

Hazel pumped her fist in the air. "Congrats! You totally

deserve it."

The look on Casey's face brightened the entire group. He grabbed the ribbon, flipping it back and forth in his hands. "That's my name on it. I really did win something."

Seeing Casey's reaction almost made up for the fact that Thomas was still at the fair as a fifth wheel. His mood instantly deflated when Hazel leaned over to Stuart.

"That's almost as good as a guinea pig ribbon," she said.

Stuart smiled at her, bumping against her side, and Thomas bristled. How did they already have inside jokes? It was time to get out of the romantic flowers and on to a different activity. Thankfully, he had years of tradition to fall back on.

"Where are we heading next?" he asked. "The petting zoo or the pie eating contest? Or did you want to try to beat my time on the mechanical bull?"

Each suggestion brought another wrinkle to Stuart's face until he was frowning like a ninety-year-old man. "Aren't we all a little too old for those activities?"

Hazel shook her head. "Not when you've been doing them for years. It wouldn't be a proper fair if we didn't do them."

"But you're a vet. How can you approve of a petting zoo? Isn't that inhumane to the animals?"

Hazel's face lit up. "I used to think so. Now I work closely with the local ranchers to make sure all the animals are rotated out and that none of them gets too stressed. It really helps a lot of the younger children in our community to get over some of their fears."

"You've already been to the petting zoo this year?"

Stuart's arms were folded across his chest.

Thomas had guessed Stuart wouldn't want to go there, and it looked like he was right. "What's wrong? It sounds like you're not a fan."

Stuart shook his head. "Okay. True confession. When I was little, I got separated from my parents while we were at the fair. I was watching the animals through the fence and one of the workers let me into the petting area with a large family."

"That's lucky," Hazel said.

"Not so much. I was doing great until a goat discovered that I had sticky ice cream on my shirt. He knocked me over and was happily sucking on my jacket while I lay there in shock. I guess the worker kept looking at my 'parents' but since they weren't doing anything, he figured I was fine. It wasn't until I was wailing in a heap on the ground that they realized I was a stranded child. By then, my favorite shirt was ruined, and my parents were nowhere to be found."

"That sounds awful," Emily said.

Even Thomas had to admit that was a pretty sad story. So much for his plan to scare Stuart away with a little bit of dirt.

"Yeah. I got a lot of ice cream cones to make up for my being stranded. I'd be happy to go with you if you need to check the animals, but I'm going to keep my distance once we get there."

Hazel looked at Thomas. "Are you okay if we skip the petting zoo this year? I can come check them out later in the week."

Stuart spoke up first. "Absolutely not. Let's go. If anything, it will probably be good for me to see the animals through the eyes of someone who really likes them."

Emily grabbed Hazel's arm, and the women talked together animatedly, leading the way with their heads tilted towards each other. It left Stuart in the back, walking next to Porter and Thomas.

"They seem to be having fun," Stuart quipped. "Planning world domination?"

Thomas couldn't hold back his smile. "That's what we used to say my sister Hope was doing whenever she'd talk to her friends. They would get such serious looks on their faces, we were afraid they were plotting to take over the world."

Porter began to laugh. "Remember the one time we caught them in the garage? I was sure they were up to no good because as soon as I opened the door, they went completely quiet."

The story was tickling a memory in the back of Thomas's mind, but he couldn't remember why. Then it hit him. He tried to shake his head discreetly at Porter, but Porter plowed on with the rest of the story, completely oblivious to his brother's signals. If Hope found out what Porter was saying, she'd never forgive him.

"That was the day we learned that Hope was part of a band. She and her friends had been performing for small groups all around town. Back then, they were mediocre at best. She and her friends got teased for years, but then she managed to turn her singing into something good."

"I can relate," Stuart said. "That's pretty much what

happened to me, except we met in J's basement instead of a garage. My mom thought I was practicing for a school event. She was shocked when she realized we were performing at our local fundraising event."

Porter's eyes widened. "Wait. You're in a band?"

"That's how I met Hazel. I was playing a gig at the Spotted Cow last week. I guess she knows our lead singer."

"What's his name?" Thomas asked. He wanted to know which one of his friends he should clobber.

"Jonah Jack. Do you know him?"

Thomas nodded. "I can't believe you know Jonah. He's a cool guy." Thomas had forgotten that Jonah was in a band. If Stuart was part of it, he was probably a better guy than Thomas was giving him credit for.

Once they got close to the petting zoo, the smell of farm animals mixed with straw assaulted Thomas's nose. Short metal fences had been wired together to form the perimeter of the petting zoo. A thick layer of straw was scattered on the ground, but dozens of feet moving in and out of the enclosure had spread the straw out onto the surrounding pavement.

Hazel glanced at Stuart. "Ready to meet some animals?"

Stuart paled. "How about I watch from here?" He leaned against the fence, his nose wrinkling against the smell.

"We'll be quick." Hazel led the way, with Emily right behind. They headed straight for a man standing right inside the enclosure. Thomas jogged after the women, reaching them in time to hear the introductions.

"Farmer Brandon, this is my friend Emily. She's newer to town."

"It's nice to meet you, Emily." He held out his hand, giving Emily's hand a big shake. "Are you here to check out the animals?"

Emily shook her head. "I have llamas. Hazel thought they might make a fun addition to your petting zoo."

Farmer Brandon's eyes crinkled. "Llamas at the petting zoo? That would be a new one for us. I'd love it, and I think the kids would too. Can I get your contact info?"

Thomas followed Hazel as she went into the enclosure to begin her routine check of the animals, leaving Emily behind with Farmer Brandon. "You taught me how to spot if they were getting dehydrated. Anything else we should be checking for this year?" He had been helping Hazel with the petting zoo for years. He wasn't about to stop because she had brought a date.

"I'm mainly checking that none of them seem too stressed out. There seems to be way more people at the fair this year than there were last year. If any of the animals seem afraid to approach you, let me know."

Thomas headed towards the goats. "Got it." He held his hand out, and one of the more curious ones immediately began to sniff him. "You guys seem just fine," he said, rubbing the chin of a small, tan goat. The goat's rough whiskers tickled his hand.

He moved on to the next animal, keeping Hazel in his peripheral vision. She was a natural with the animals, moving between them as if she was telling them an exciting story that they all wanted to hear. Hazel's entire body relaxed when she was surrounded by animals, even if they were pushing against the backs of her knees.

One particularly excited goat ran to Hazel, knocking her forward in his attempts to reach the grain in her hands. Thomas ran to her side, steadying her shoulder before she crashed to the ground. He held on until she was stable.

"Thanks," Hazel said, but she couldn't meet his eye.

Thomas stood back, confusion flickering through his mind. Why was she acting strange? She never had a problem looking him straight in the face. In fact, there were many days where she had gotten to the root of Thomas's problems because she refused to look away. Why would this day be any different?

Then Thomas remembered Stuart. He had spent the day annoyed with the tag-along date, but Thomas hadn't stopped to consider that Hazel might really like the guy. Her reaction to his touch put everything in perspective.

Traditions or not, Thomas wasn't sure how much longer he could stay at the fair. His stomach sank. There was no way he could stick around, watching the woman of his dreams fall in love with another guy. That would hurt too much, even for the tough rancher.

Thomas cleared his throat and turned to finish his assessment. Even the small rabbits hopping in their enclosure did nothing to lift his mood. He watched, disinterested, as a small girl with golden curls bent down to pet one of the bunnies. Her beaming smile was a painful reminder of the days when he was the one who made Hazel smile.

The churning in his stomach intensified, shifting from

jealousy to an actual ache. If he didn't get out of the petting zoo soon, the contents of his stomach were going to erupt all over the fresh straw.

"I'll be back," Thomas called. He made a beeline for the bathroom, pushing his way to the nearest trash can. Throwing up at home with a nice warm bed to climb into was one thing. Throwing up with an audience? That was something Thomas could do without.

A sharp pain shot through his stomach and Thomas doubled over again. When he straightened up, sweat trickled down the back of his neck. He knew something was wrong when the room started spinning.

Thomas slid down by the side of the trash can, not caring how disgusting the ground was. He pressed his head between his knees, willing the room to stay still.

"Are you okay, mister?" a voice asked, but Thomas was too far gone to hear.

He closed his eyes and tried to focus on something other than his nausea. The world was spinning sideways when Thomas opened his eyes again. He was surrounded by boots, but none of them were doing anything to take away the stabbing pain in his side.

He thought he heard Porter calling his name, but it was too late. He was slipping away, his mind shutting down. As always, the last thought on his mind was Hazel.

She was smoothing his hair to the side, whispering to him that he was okay. He wanted to snuggle into her arms and hold her close, apologizing that he had been such a jerk, but his words wouldn't come out. He tried to speak, and the world went dark.

CHAPTER 8

The chill of the hospital room seemed to fit the sparse decor, with bright fluorescent lights illuminating the machines at the head of Thomas's bed. Hazel hadn't left Thomas's side in hours. She pulled her chair next to the side of his bed, keeping watch while his mom and siblings filed in and out, taking their turns beside her.

There were more comfortable couches in the waiting room, a fact that each Matthews family member mentioned when they came to take their turn on the hard plastic chair next to Hazel. It didn't matter to her. She had seen how pale Thomas's face was when the paramedics carried him out of the bathroom on the stretcher. The color was coming back, but she wasn't leaving until he opened his eyes.

Hazel was pretty sure Stuart thought she was crazy when she had barged into the men's restroom behind Porter. She didn't care. A friend had texted Porter that his brother was down, and he went running, with Hazel right behind.

It didn't take medical training to see that something was very wrong. The sheen on Thomas's forehead hadn't been normal, but the most concerning part was his inability to speak. He murmured Hazel's name once before going completely limp.

Sitting in the hospital room, Hazel knew she was done dancing around the issue of whether Thomas cared about her or not. She was going to ask him to try having a relationship no matter what the risks were of getting rejected.

Emily arrived to take her turn keeping watch. She pressed a fresh cup of coffee into Hazel's hands. "Any changes?" she asked.

Hazel shook her head. "I don't know why he hasn't woken up yet, but the doctor says it is normal." She took a sip of the coffee and set it on the tray table beside her.

"It was his appendix?" Emily swapped seats with Reid, nodding goodbye before he left to join his family in the waiting room.

"Yeah. It was so inflamed, it burst while the doctors were taking it out."

Thomas stirred and Hazel froze, watching to see if he was waking up. His eyelids fluttered as if trying to open them was a heavy task. Then they closed and his breathing slowed back to a steady rhythm.

Her mind struggled to make sense of the scene in front of her. In all her years of knowing Thomas, she had never seen him weak. He pushed through to finish his work, whether he was limping, feverish or just so tired he could barely stand. He always showed up, and now he couldn't even open his eyes.

Emily rested her hand on Hazel's arm, pulling her out of her thoughts. "I'm sure he's going to be okay. It's a common surgery that millions of people get every year."

"It's really dangerous if the appendix ruptures. What if an infection spreads? That can kill people." Hazel's thoughts were spiraling downwards as they raced through worst case scenarios.

Why had she wasted her last moments with Thomas by bringing a silly date to the fair? Stuart had been nice enough, but sitting in the hospital room with Thomas, she knew that her heart needed to follow this relationship through, even if it ended in heartache. She pushed her chair back and began to pace.

"Emily, what if the last thing he remembers is me hanging out with a different guy? I don't want him to think it was something serious."

"You really like him, don't you?" Emily said.

Hazel glanced at Thomas where all his worry lines were smoothed out while he slept. "I always have." She turned to look at her friend's face before settling back into her chair. "I'm scared though. What if he doesn't feel the same, and I mess up our friendship? He's too important to lose."

Emily clasped her hands together and rested them on the edge of the bed. "Are you kidding? Were you paying any attention at the fair?"

"To what?"

"To the way Thomas was acting. I thought he was going

to have a heart attack when he saw you standing there with Stuart. Were you trying to get under his skin?"

"No. I was just trying to do something so my mind wasn't constantly fixated on him. Was he actually jealous?" He had been acting so normal, doing all their favorite things. Emily's words didn't make sense.

"I wasn't jealous," Thomas muttered, shifting in his bed. "I can take him in an arm-wrestling match."

Tears sprung to Hazel's eyes as she stood up from her chair. "You're awake."

"Yeah."

"How are you feeling?" She gave his hand a squeeze before gently stroking his arm.

Emily stood. "I'll give you guys a minute alone before I tell the rest of the family."

Thomas watched her leave, but he didn't say anything. Then he turned to Hazel.

"I feel like I got punched by a truck. What happened?"

Hazel pulled her hand back and sank into her chair, causing a large frown to appear on Thomas's face.

"Why did you do that?" he asked.

"Do what?"

"I liked your hand where it was." He flipped his hand over, so his palm was up. "Can I have it back, please?"

Hazel's heart leaped. There was a chance he felt the same way she did, or he could still be groggy from the medicine. It didn't matter either way. She slid her hand into his, curling her fingers around his wrist with one hand while she stroked his arm with the other. "Better?"

Thomas lifted her hand to his lips and gave it a soft kiss. "Much better."

The feeling of safety that shot through Hazel's body surprised her. She looked into her friend's eyes, holding his gaze. "I agree." His fingers wrapped around hers felt so right, she wondered why they hadn't been holding hands for years.

"You gave us a scare back there," Hazel said.

Thomas stretched his head from side to side, looking around the room. "I still don't know what happened."

"I can answer that," a deep voice said. The doctor walked into the room, coming to a stop beside Thomas's bed while he flipped through a chart. "The short answer is that you had appendicitis. Had you been having pain throughout the day?"

Thomas glanced Hazel's way before he looked at the ceiling. "Maybe just a little."

"And you didn't think you should get it looked at?" Hazel asked. She glared at him.

"We were at the fair," he finally said. Hazel could fill in the pieces. Thomas was busy watching her with Stuart. She couldn't stand that he had been toughing it out to try to impress her.

Thomas gave Hazel's hand a reassuring squeeze. "I have a high pain tolerance, and I didn't think it was a big deal. I honestly thought that it was something I ate. I can handle a stomachache."

This was the Thomas that Hazel knew. The one who would work through any discomfort to finish the job. The

Thomas in the bed in front of her was unfamiliar, but she liked seeing his vulnerable side.

"When can he go home?" Mom Matthews asked. She came into the room, leaning over the bed to give Thomas a kiss on the forehead. "I'm glad to see you awake."

Hazel's cheeks flushed and she tried to slip her hand out of Thomas's, but he tightened his grip. She had been kidding herself if she thought the family wouldn't notice her attraction to Thomas, but she was hoping to keep it to herself until she could understand her own feelings.

Pages rustled as the doctor flipped back to the first page of the chart. Then he turned to the computer, clicking a few buttons. "We plan to keep you here for a couple of days to make sure we catch any infection."

Thomas struggled to sit up. "I don't have time for that."

"Yes, you do," Reid called out.

Hazel glanced at the door, smiling when she saw all the siblings crowding around the small opening. The hospital had requested that only two guests visit at a time, but they didn't say anything about lurking in the hallway. It wasn't fair for Hazel to be hogging up one of the spots now that Thomas was awake.

She tried to pull away, but Thomas tightened his grip. "Will you stop doing that?" he asked, staring pointedly at her hand.

"Your family wants to see you. I was going to let them take my spot."

Thomas frowned. He looked at his mom and then back at Hazel. "You are fine where you are, right guys?" He raised his voice for the last part of the question, glancing towards the door where his siblings were all nodding their heads.

Mom Matthews patted Hazel's shoulder. "It's okay. We're pretty good at taking turns. You stay where you are."

Hazel could feel the flush of embarrassment creeping up her cheeks. She looked at Thomas, and the vulnerability on his face broke her shell. "I'm not going anywhere," she told him.

He kissed her hand again. "Thank you."

* * *

HAZEL WASN'T sure what to expect the following day. When she went home to sleep, Thomas was alert and talking. All Hazel wanted was a moment alone with him to talk about their relationship, but the number of siblings surrounding him made that pretty much impossible.

She arrived at his room the following morning and found Bree perched on the end of his bed. Hazel was going to make a quip about him needing his rest until she watched the way his eyes lit up when he spoke to his sister. As the baby of the family, Bree had all the siblings wrapped around her pinky finger.

Her face lit up when Hazel walked into the room. "Finally. This guy won't stop asking about you."

Thomas groaned and covered his face. "Smooth, Bree."

"It's okay," Hazel said. "I feel the same way. I tried to get here sooner but I had to take care of a couple of things at the clinic."

Bree grimaced. "It doesn't matter what took you so

long. Now that you're here, you can help me pick my homecoming dress." She pulled out her phone and swiped between pictures, showing each one to Hazel.

There was an undercurrent of unspoken words between Thomas and Hazel, but Hazel decided it didn't matter. She pulled her chair close and placed her hand in Thomas's outstretched grip, and then settled into the conversation with Bree.

Some of the dresses Bree showed her were awful. One of them was chartreuse with a neckline that plunged to the belly button. It could be a red-carpet look, but not something for a high school senior. Bree shifted so she was sitting against the small foot of the bed, her legs folded beneath her. "It's nice having a sister here again."

A sister? Hazel stiffened, wondering what Thomas had been saying to Bree. Seeming to sense the shift of energy in the room, Bree caught herself.

"I mean, another girl. My mom tries to help but I think she'd put me in a floor length, long-sleeved dress with a high neck. And Hope isn't much help off at college. She thinks her homework is more important than looking at dresses."

Hazel chuckled, but her heart liked the thought of being a sister to Bree. If she started dating Thomas, she'd get to be around a large family. That was something she missed growing up with just one brother and one sister.

They had narrowed down the dress selection when Reid poked his head into the room. "My turn, Little Sis. Don't you have to be at school?" He pulled the tray table close to the bed and pulled out a deck of cards while Bree gathered her things.

Bree rolled her eyes at Reid. "Thanks for the help, Hazel. Will you be here later?"

Hazel glanced at Thomas, who nodded his head. "I think so. I can stay if there aren't too many animal emergencies."

Bree gave her a quick hug. "He's not as grumpy when you're here," she whispered. Then she straightened up. "Bye guys."

The slap of cards on the tray table replaced the chatter about homecoming dresses, and Hazel settled in. It looked like she wasn't going to get her moment alone with Thomas any time soon. She would have to be patient.

The alone time never came. Hazel's heart swirled with unspoken questions, but there was always another Matthews family member keeping watch to make sure Thomas was okay. By the third day, Hazel had to get back to her office. The neighboring vet was inundated with more calls than he could handle.

Thomas went home when Hazel was bandaging a gash on a horse's leg. She felt bad she couldn't be there but holding hands and sitting in a hospital room wasn't real life. She had patients who needed her.

CHAPTER 9

A foul mood followed Thomas home from the hospital. He had hated being cooped up in a small recovery room all day, but now that he was back on the ranch, still grounded from doing any heavy lifting, he was getting impatient. It was embarrassing having to ask the neighbors to pitch in and help with the animals while he recovered.

On top of not feeling well, he was missing Hazel. She said she was busy, but he was second guessing every conversation they had had. At the hospital, Hazel was a beam of light in the room. Holding her hand felt proper, like it was something he had forgotten he was supposed to be doing. She fit in with his family with an ease that surprised him. Any woman that could hold her own surrounded by his siblings deserved his respect.

It would be easy to pretend that holding hands with Hazel didn't mean anything, but Thomas couldn't deny his feelings. Touching her soft skin sent waves of longing through his body. He wanted more than the glimpses of what a relationship could bring. He wanted it all.

To make matters worse, Porter and Emily were nearing their six-month anniversary. He knew it was only a matter of time before Porter proposed and Thomas was left behind. A caring brother would be happy that Porter was getting everything he wanted in life, but Thomas's foul mood wasn't letting him enjoy that happiness. Instead, he bristled every time he saw how naturally Porter and Emily fit together.

The way Thomas saw it, he either had to give dating Hazel a real try, or he had to relocate to another state until Porter and Emily stopped being so sickly sweet together.

Thomas was throwing a ball at the family room wall when Reid found him.

"Having fun there?" Reid asked.

The answering scowl was all the answer Thomas could summon. He threw the ball one more time, catching it on the return. Then he tossed it to Reid.

"Do you ever hate being alone?" Thomas asked.

"I'm not sure I'm following you." Reid sat on the arm of a large, overstuffed sofa. "We have so many people coming and going, I don't think it's ever quiet here."

"I'm not talking about people in the house. I'm talking about dating."

Reid rolled the ball back and forth between his hands. "Got it. Did you spend a little too much time with Porter and Emily at the hospital? I thought you were happy being a bachelor."

"I was," Thomas said. He kicked against the edge of the

couch, looking for an outlet for his frustration. "I was totally okay being alone. I was going to take care of the ranch and mom. We all were. I figured I'd get my chance at love later."

"But then Porter had to ruin it," Reid said.

"Yeah." Thomas was twisting inside, his emotions winding tighter and tighter until he was afraid he was going to explode.

"And maybe Hazel had to go and ruin it too?" Reid asked. He tossed a pillow towards his brother. "This definitely isn't the conversation of someone who is content with being single anymore."

His brother had a point, which made Thomas more upset. "A deal is a deal. Take care of the ranch. Take care of mom."

Like a bat with super hearing, Mom Matthews came into the room. "Who is taking care of me?" she asked.

"Me," Thomas said. And Reid and Porter. Hudson and Hope too. We made a pact."

"I see." Mom slid her hands into her jeans pockets. "Were any of you going to ask me what I thought about this pact?"

"We didn't have to," Reid said. "You lost dad, and we weren't going to make you handle everything on your own."

Thomas held his breath. They were telling their mom a secret that they had sworn to keep, no matter what. The siblings knew she wouldn't like being taken care of, but it was obvious she had needed the help back then.

She sat on the couch next to Thomas. "I love your giant

hearts, and I love that you are trying to watch out for me, but maybe it's time to change your pact."

"What do you mean?" Thomas asked.

"I mean, you are all older now. I was drowning when I lost your father. I barely knew which way was up, and there was no way I could handle taking over a ranch while trying to raise a family. Bree was only ten."

"That's why we made the pact," Reid said.

Mom held up her hand. "Let me finish." She picked up a small notebook from the side table. "This is my list of things I want to accomplish. Look at the first item."

Thomas read it to himself, and then out loud to Reid. "Raise confident children who will follow their dreams and make a difference in the world."

"I write that sentence at the top of the page every day. I feel honored that I was blessed with children who were responsible enough to take care of me. I also want you to recognize that things have shifted. I'm not a struggling widow anymore."

The door swung open, and Porter's voice boomed through the hall. "I'm home. Where is everyone?"

"In here," Reid called.

Porter bounded into the room with a smile on his face that was about to be taken away.

"Mom found out about our pact," Thomas said.

Porter folded his arms across his chest, looking back and forth between his brothers. "Seriously?" A scowl creased his brow.

"Yeah," Reid said. "She's not too happy with us."

Thomas glanced at his mom, who was shaking her head

from side to side. The scowl on her face spoke volumes. She held her hands out.

"It's not that I'm unhappy with you. If anything, it makes me kind of sad that I didn't notice."

Mom pointed at Porter. "Please tell me you haven't been holding back in dating Emily because of this pact."

Porter shook his head. "I'm taking things slow with Emily because I've been married before. I want to make sure it is right before I commit to forever."

The look she gave Porter made Thomas glad he wasn't on the receiving end of it. "And it has nothing to do with your promise to your brothers?"

Porter shifted from side to side. "Maybe in the beginning. I was a little worried about the pact, but once I fell in love, I figured we'd work it out."

"I'm glad. I know how happy Emily makes you. If you were holding back because of me, it would break my heart."

Thomas watched the interchange, trying to keep his mouth shut. Sure, Porter could date someone and leave the ranch, but that meant more responsibility for everyone else. Why could he back out of the pact without worrying about the consequences?

Mom stood, ruffling the hair on Thomas's head. "I've got to get back to the kitchen. Thank you for taking care of me so well. As of now, can we dissolve this pact?"

Reid and Porter exchanged glances. "I guess," Reid said.

She looked at Thomas. "That means you, too."

Thomas curled his fingers into fists. It was easy to say yes, they'd drop it, but someone still had to be responsible for the ranch. The way Porter was grinning, Thomas guessed he was more than ready to walk away. The heaviness of responsibility settled on Thomas's shoulders but he wasn't going to let his mom down.

"Of course, Mom." They were the words she wanted to hear, but Thomas didn't mean them. He'd have to figure out a new way to make sure she was taken care of.

His brothers filed out of the room after their mom, leaving Thomas with his swirling thoughts. He slouched down against the cushions, wondering how he was going to handle his responsibilities. Reid and Porter may be willing to leave their mom in a lurch, but that wasn't something Thomas could do.

Thomas opened the window, letting in a crisp breeze that helped to clear his mind. If he was going to be in a bad mood, he was going to drive everyone in the family crazy. They didn't deserve that after taking such good care of him. It was time to change the mood.

Thomas picked up his phone and dialed Hazel's number. His heart fluttered when she answered, the sound of her voice a welcome balm to his troubled thoughts.

"Hi," he said. He wiped a hand on his jeans, feeling suddenly tongue tied. If his dad was around, he'd give Thomas a stern lecture about letting fear dictate his future. "I was wondering if I could take you out sometime this week. On a real date."

The words were out. Thomas usually danced around the idea of a date, calling it a hang out or a group thing. But now he was asking directly. It was time to figure out if he and Hazel could be a couple.

Her voice was light when she answered. "I'd really like that. What does your schedule look like?"

"Well, it's pretty packed trying to give proper lounge attention to every couch in the house. And then, after dinner, I have some dishes to wash."

Hazel laughed, the sound lifting his spirits. "Sorry. I forgot you're recovering. It looks like I might finish early at the clinic today. Does tonight work?"

Gulping, Thomas nodded. Then he used his words. "Tonight would be perfect."

"Do you want me to swing by after work and pick you up? I'm not sure what your driving restrictions are."

She was thoughtful, as always, yet the idea of needing help with just one more thing made him bristle. "I'm cleared for driving. How about I come grab you whenever you're ready?"

"It's a date," Hazel said.

She hung up the phone and Thomas walked to his room. He was exhausted now that the conversation was over. With the hardest part out of the way, Thomas had to figure out where they were going to go.

THOMAS THOUGHT he understood how slowly a day could pass, but he had underestimated the boredom of being on his own ranch; his body holding him back from working. He was on strict no-lifting orders for three more days, which sounded doable when the doctor told him to take it easy. The reality, however, was that he was absolutely stir-crazy.

There wasn't a lot Thomas could do on the ranch but he had tried to be helpful. He had collected chicken eggs, helped with the cooking, and made an inventory of all the tractor supplies they might need, but those tasks had only filled part of his day.

Talking to the horses filled another hour. He wasn't allowed to ride, and heavy lifting was a definite no-no, so he had to settle for walking from field to field to see how they were doing. According to his reconnaissance, the horses were well-fed and content. Even old Sunflower, his dad's favorite horse, was meandering around the field. She didn't move as fast as she had before the arthritis set in, but she was still able to run through the fields with the other horses.

Thomas even checked the garden, stooping to pull a few weeds that had crept up in the tomato bed. He had never felt so useless. If this was what getting old felt like, Thomas wasn't sure he'd be able to handle it.

The sun wasn't even thinking about setting when Thomas headed in to get ready for his date. He took a shower and then took the time to perfectly style his hair. He pulled out a soft green t-shirt, wincing slightly as he lifted his hands above his head to pull the shirt over. Maybe there was something to be said for the doctor's orders.

Thomas came to the family room and sank to the sofa while family members cycled in and out of the house. Somewhere between Bree complaining about her math homework and Porter talking on the phone to Emily, Thomas drifted off to sleep.

He jolted upright when his mom lay a blanket over his shoulders. "What time is it?" he asked, confused by the setting sun.

"It's a little after seven. I figured your body needed the rest. Do you want me to heat you up a plate of food?"

"Not yet. Thanks, mom."

Thomas glanced at his phone; anxious he had missed Hazel's call. The screen was blank, which meant that something must have come up. He didn't start worrying until it got close to eight. He wanted to call, but he knew Hazel. She would text when she was ready.

When Hazel called at 8:37, her voice was rough. She sounded like she had been crying.

"What's wrong?" Thomas asked.

Hazel sniffled. "I lost a foal."

The words punched Thomas in the heart. He knew that Hazel took each loss personally. "I'm so sorry. What can I do?" He pulled on a boot, eager to give her a hug and help her decompress.

"Is it okay if we postpone our date to another day?" Hazel asked.

Thomas paused, the second boot still in his hand. How was he supposed to take care of Hazel if he couldn't even see her?

"Of course." Thomas hung up the phone, feeling as if the entire day had been a waste. He hadn't been able to help on the ranch, and now he couldn't even help Hazel.

Thomas was pulling his boots off when he changed his

mind. Hazel said she wasn't up for a date, but that didn't mean she didn't want to see him. He knew just the right peace offering to get him in the door.

"Bye," he called to the quiet house, knowing the family was all nearby.

"Have fun on your date," Mom called back.

"Don't do anything I wouldn't do," Reid yelled.

Thomas grinned. It wasn't going to be a date, and it wasn't going to be fun, but Thomas knew he'd rather be holding Hazel than sitting home alone. The mission to lift Hazel's spirits was on.

CHAPTER 10

*L*eaving the Johnson farm had been heartbreaking. Mr. Johnson was barely holding it together, and his youngest daughter was in tears. Unfortunately, they had called Hazel too late. By the time she arrived at the ranch, the mare was already in severe distress. Hazel tried an emergency c-section, but she hadn't been confident she could save the baby.

She was right. The beautiful foal had no heartbeat by the time Hazel was able to extract him. Hazel wished that her job as a vet came with superpowers, but her lifesaving skills were no match for a delivery that had stalled hours before. A seasoned rancher would have called sooner, but the Johnsons were still learning the ropes.

Hazel tried her best to comfort the family, but her words sounded hollow even to her own ears. In all her years of working with animals, she had still never found words that would comfort a grieving family. The best she could do was to promise to check in on the mare the following day. They already lost one horse. There was no reason to make it two.

Driving home, she wasn't sure what to do about her date with Thomas. It was something that should have filled her with excitement, but her emotional capacity to deal with people was empty. There was no way she could handle being in a crowded restaurant, so she called Thomas to cancel.

After hanging up the phone, her heart felt emptier than before. Not only had she failed to save the foal, but now she was turning away the friendship and conversation she desperately needed.

It was going to be an early pajama and movie night for sure.

Hazel was pulling on her soft fleece leggings when someone rang the doorbell. Her spirits fell. Why was there always an interruption when she was trying to get settled after a long day of work? She reached for her closest t-shirt, pulling it on while she slowly walked towards the door. Hopefully, if she took long enough, the person would give up and go away.

No such luck. The doorbell rang again, this time accompanied by a loud knocking.

"I'm coming," Hazel called. She mustered a smile and turned the knob, pulling the door open a small crack.

Thomas stood on the doorstep, looking breathtakingly handsome wearing a green shirt that made the color of his eyes pop. Hazel glanced down at her torn band t-shirt, a slight heat rising on her cheeks. He could have stepped off the runway and she looked like the poster child for a clothing donation center. Scratch that. Even the center wouldn't take her outfit.

She detected a glimmer of hope in Thomas's eyes when he held out the plastic bag. "I know you said no date, but I figured you probably hadn't eaten anything yet. I brought you some Hawaiian pulled pork and macaroni salad."

"From Joe's Hula Barn?" The smell wafting up from the bag was undeniably heavenly.

"I know your favorite place to eat."

Tears pricked Hazel's eyes as she swung the door all the way open. She stepped out and wrapped her arms around his waist, burying her face in his chest. Thomas rubbed her back, smoothing down her hair while he gently rocked her back and forth.

Thomas was what she needed to make the night better. Not a stupid movie or comfy pajama pants.

"How did you know?" Hazel asked.

"Your favorite restaurant? We've been there a bunch of times."

"No. How did you know I'd need you tonight?" She pushed back so she could meet his gaze. His hazel and green flecked eyes studied her, while the last rays of the setting sun cast dark shadows on his face.

Thomas brushed the hair out of her eyes. "I was hoping that you needed me as much as I've been needing you all day. I missed you."

With that, Hazel's heart split wide open. She pulled him into her house and closed the door behind him. Her spirits were already lighter.

"I hope you brought enough dinner for two."

* * *

AN HOUR LATER, the bad day was wiped from Hazel's mind. She was curled up on the couch against Thomas's side, happy shivers racing through her body every time he stroked her arm. His arm around her shoulders was heavy but comforting.

There were conversations that needed to happen, but Hazel wasn't sure she wanted to break her happy bubble. The way things stood, she was standing on the brink of a friendship with a man she'd known for years, ready to jump into an epic love story. If he was the right man for her, she guessed the relationship would progress quickly.

Hazel knew what her body wanted in regard to physical touch. She was a snuggler, and she knew that she liked snuggling with Thomas quite a lot. She had also really enjoyed holding his hand in the hospital. Was it enough though? Was holding hands with Thomas a good enough reason to justify changing a twelve-year friendship?

Thomas shifted slightly, causing Hazel to sink further into his arms. He was a rock she relied on, and the person she could always turn to, good day or bad. He had been there for her the day Danny fell into the pond. He held her hand at the funeral when the entire world was capsizing around her. He was also there for her when she had to check her dad into a care center because his Alzheimer's had progressed to a point that he was no longer able to care for himself. Thomas had wiped away more of Hazel's tears than she could count, but he had done it as a friend.

She pulled her knees up so her legs were crisscrossed on the couch.

"What's on your mind?" Thomas asked.

Hazel's mind was screaming at her to slow down. There were plenty of ways to answer the question, but Hazel was too tired of dancing around the issue.

"Why haven't we dated before?" she asked.

Thomas stiffened beside her, his breath hitching for a second before he relaxed. "Lots of reasons."

"That's not really an answer." Hazel sat up and turned so she was facing him directly. "I'm serious. Sitting on the couch with your arm around me feels as natural to me as breathing. So why don't we do it all the time?"

Thomas rested his hand on her knee. "Would you believe me if I said it's because your house is a mess?" He picked up a sock from the edge of the couch and waved it in front of her face.

"Nope. I'm pretty sure you have seen my messy house before." The sink was filled with unwashed dishes, waiting for a free minute for Hazel to wash them. She hadn't gotten to the laundry either. Spending all her time with Thomas at the hospital combined with working overtime had definitely affected her motivation to clean up.

"You want the truth?" Thomas locked eyes with her and a different tremble went through her body. This was the conversation she had been longing to have, and now that it was here, she was terrified.

"Yes please," Hazel said.

Thomas pulled his knee up so he was sitting sideways on the couch, facing Hazel more directly. "We've been friends for so long, I didn't want to ruin things. Honestly, I wanted to ask you out our senior year. When that didn't happen, I decided to accept the friendship for what it was."

Hazel's mouth dropped open. "No you didn't. You were dating Lisa."

Thomas ran a hand through his hair. "Yeah. I asked her out because you had been talking about that football player you said was so cute."

Hazel wracked her memory, but she couldn't remember any such guy. "Are you sure?"

He nodded. "It was a month before the big homecoming game. I was trying to get my courage up to ask you out and then you came into English class one day, stars in your eyes. You told me all about the new foreign exchange student in your class, and how cute he was. He was on the football team, and you couldn't wait to cheer him on at the big game."

"Oh my gosh. Eowen. I had forgotten all about him."

"Well, I never did. Instead of asking you to the dance, I asked Lisa. When things ended badly with her, I knew I wasn't ready to risk our friendship by trying to date you."

Hazel clasped her hands in front of her. "So, I have a confession. There was no actual new student named Eowen. I was telling you about a character on one of my favorite shows. I thought if I made you jealous, you'd ask me to the dance so he couldn't." She could feel the laughter welling up. "I guess that backfired in a big way."

Thomas rolled his eyes at the ceiling before pinning her down with a glare. Then he smirked. "You made him up?"

"Yeah." Hazel scooted closer so her knees were touching

his. "I did it because I wanted to go to the dance with you, but it backfired in a big way. I had to accept a date with Leonard Hall instead."

"And then he stood you up."

Hazel could still feel the rejection. "The whole time we were at the dance, I wished I was there with you."

"Huh." Thomas grinned. "I guess you kind of were my date."

"That doesn't count. You and Lisa were so sweet to try to take care of me but watching you guys fall in love made the dance awful. I couldn't stop crying all night."

A look of understanding flashed across Thomas's face. He reached for her hands. "I was stupid back then. I couldn't see what was right in front of me."

His touch sent sparks that raced through her body. "I was pretty dumb back then, too. So where does that leave us now?" Hazel waited for him to answer. She had made a lot of assumptions about how Thomas felt in the past. Now it was time to listen to what he had to say.

"I'm not sure." Thomas slid his hand up Hazel's arm and she leaned into his touch. "I know that I need you in my life. I value our friendship too much to let that go." He caressed the side of her cheek, igniting the sparks in her heart to full flames. "I also know that I can't really go back to just hugging you on occasion or putting my arm around you as a casual friend."

Hazel's spirit was soaring, floating out of her body while she listened to his words.

"How do you feel about trying to date? We could see how it works out." Thomas asked.

Hazel grinned. "So, like, are you asking me to be your girlfriend?" She clasped her hands together, holding them in front of her body.

He tossed his head back and ran a hand through his hair. "Like, I guess maybe."

Hazel reached for his hand, wrapping her fingers through it as she leaned close. "Then I guess my answer is yes."

An endearing grin spread across his face. Hazel tried to take a snapshot in her mind. She was trying to capture the picture when the expression in his eyes changed. Hazel barely had time to register what was happening when Thomas began to lean forward.

Three things flashed across her mind in quick succession. The first was that Thomas Matthews looked a lot like a man who was about to kiss his best friend. The second was that she was pretty sure she was going to implode from happiness the second his lips touched hers. The third was to wonder if she'd have the will power to stop kissing Thomas once she started.

Hazel sighed when he slid his hand to the back of her neck, fingers combing through her hair. For a kiss that had been overdue for years, the anticipation was driving her crazy. She parted her lips, preparing for the moment when their lips would meet. The bad night had definitely turned around, in the best sort of way.

As she started to close her eyes, a shrill ring pierced the air. It took Hazel a second to register where the sound was coming from, but Thomas was already pulling away, the moment shattered. She wanted to throw her phone across the room, but Hazel knew the sound of the after-hours ringtone. There was an animal in distress somewhere, and she wasn't going to let it be hurt because she really wanted to try kissing her best friend.

"Hi Jana," Hazel said. "What's the emergency?" She jumped to her feet as Jana filled her in on the details, running to her bedroom to change into work clothes.

Thomas was waiting when she came out. "Something serious?" he asked.

"A dog ran into the freeway, and someone hit it." She remembered the time she thought she had hit Scully. "It's hurt pretty badly but Jana thinks I can save it."

Thomas reached for his hat. "Do you want me to come with you?" he asked.

Hazel shook her head. "I'm heading straight to surgery." She placed a hand on his cheek, her heart aching at the abrupt ending to the night.

"Can we pick this up later?" she asked.

Thomas's low voice sent a small shiver of delight through her body when he answered. "I can't wait."

Then she was out the door, her lips tingling with anticipation of the kiss to come.

CHAPTER 11

Thomas wasn't sure if he wanted to throw his hat to the ground and stomp on it for being interrupted or if he wanted to lead a stadium full of people in a cheer. Talking to Hazel had cleared all the worries from his heart. He had a girlfriend. The words danced through his mind, feeling so childish in one way, but also so right.

He had almost kissed her. The blood raced through his body when he thought about how close he had come to finally making the relationship official. He didn't kiss his friends, but he most definitely kissed girlfriends. Once they crossed that line, there would be no turning back.

Thomas held his hat to his chest, letting the brisk air clear his thoughts. Hazel had run out the door, asking him to lock up behind them. He was going to, but then he remembered that his keys were inside on the table.

A shiver of happiness ran up his spine. There had been an almost kiss, but before that, there had been a really great conversation. If the relationship with Hazel was only about the physical touch, it would be fiery and consuming, but it wouldn't last.

A relationship founded on the level of friendship they had? He knew it was going to feel different than anything he'd experienced before. He sank down on the couch, basking in his happiness for a moment longer.

If Hazel was right, her surgery was going to take a few hours. By the time she got home, it would be well past bedtime. He couldn't be there to greet her, but he wanted to do something that would leave her with a smile.

The end table gave him the idea he needed. The Styrofoam containers from dinner were pushed to the side, along with their silverware and napkins. It would take just a few seconds to clean them up. Thomas carried the containers to the kitchen to throw them away, but the trash was overflowing. That wasn't like Hazel.

With a pang, Thomas realized a lot of her clutter was probably from spending hours of her time at the hospital taking care of him. He had monopolized all her time, so she was probably behind at both work and home. He pushed down on the overflowing trash bag so he could tie the drawstrings together. Then he carried the bag out to the dumpster.

When he grabbed a clean liner from under the sink, he realized just how piled up her dishes were. Hazel's house was a little cluttered at times, but she didn't normally live like this.

In a flash, Thomas knew what he could do. He pulled open the dishwasher and got to work. His doctor had grounded him from ranch work, but he hadn't said anything about housework.

Hazel was going to be mad at Thomas for doing her dishes. He could already hear her lecture, which would involve phrases like "I don't need help" and "I was going to get to them". He also knew that when she woke up the next morning, her day would go better because her kitchen was clean.

Mom Matthews had drilled the value of a clean kitchen into her children from the time they were old enough to help. Thomas still remembered how big he felt the first time he was able to help wash the pans after dinner. It was exciting to work back then. Now it was part of regular life.

There really wasn't a lot to do in Hazel's kitchen. He was finished wiping off the counters and table in no time at all. When he stood back, a wave of satisfaction flowed through him. All that was left was the note he needed to write.

That was a little trickier. He chewed on the end of the pen, trying to think of words that weren't too cheesy and weren't too formal. Finally, he settled for the truth.

Thanks for spending time with me today. I can't wait to see you again.

Thomas tapped the pen against the paper, trying to decide what else to say. There were so many things on his mind, but they were conversations he wanted to have in person. He looked at the paper once more, grinning as he added a large heart. Then he signed his name.

* * *

THOMAS DIDN'T HEAR from Hazel until the next morning. He was replacing the dead plants in the flower bed with fresh ones when she called.

She had a sleepy rasp to her voice even though Thomas knew she'd been at work for a few hours already. "You're in trouble, mister."

"Oh really? Why is that?" Thomas straightened up, setting the trowel to the side. He rubbed his hands together to wipe off the extra dirt.

"You stayed at my house after I left. I think that's trespassing."

Thomas laughed. He couldn't even begin to count the number of times he'd been invited into Hazel's house. He even knew where she hid the spare key. "Yeah. I left my car keys inside. And then I got distracted."

"Yeah. About that. Thanks for doing the dishes. You didn't have to."

"I know, but you seemed a little overwhelmed with work. Besides, it felt good being able to do something useful instead of moping around." He really was glad he had been able to help.

Hazel was quiet for a minute. "When do I get to see you again?"

Thomas looked at the flower bed behind him, and the rows of flowers waiting to be planted. He did a quick calculation in his mind for how long it would take to finish the job. "When is your lunch break?"

"Hold on," Hazel said. There were muffled voices on the other end of the phone and then Hazel was back. "Jana says I should have a window at 12:30, but it might be short."

"I'll take it." Thomas was happy to get any time with Hazel, even if it was just for a half hour. He wanted to know how her surgery had gone.

"Alright. I'd better get back to my patients. I'll see you for lunch." Hazel hung up the phone, and Thomas picked up the next pot of flowers.

He finished planting with a half hour to spare. It was just enough time to get washed up and out the door.

Hazel's veterinarian clinic was on an acre of property that ran along the edge of town. Tall trees grew on either side of the road, standing like guards to the property. The main office was at the front of a small building. Thomas knew that several of Hazel's patients ended up recovering in the barns nearby.

Thomas's stomach sank when he pulled into the parking lot. Judging from the number of cars still parked there, it didn't look like Hazel was going to be ready to leave any time soon.

The first thing Thomas noticed when he opened the door was the sound of laughter. Not just laughter between a couple of friends, but enough laughter to fill the office. Jana wasn't at her desk in the lobby, so Thomas followed the sound of the laughter to one of the back rooms.

When he walked in, he had to rub his eyes to try to make sense of what he was seeing. The room was filled with adults and small children who were spaced out across the floor. In one corner, a group of kids were sitting in a circle around Jana, who held a parakeet on her finger. A woman Thomas vaguely recognized stood by the sink, helping children to wash their hands. Hazel sat in the middle of the chaos, her face a true reflection of joy.

"Mister. Watch out," a small voice called.

Thomas looked down in time to see a small kitten making a run for the open doorway. "Not so fast, little one," he said. He scooped the kitten out of danger and then, after carefully checking that no more animals were trying to escape, he closed the door.

Hazel was watching him with a bemused expression on her face. "You're early," she said.

The kitten was wriggling in Thomas's hands. He walked over to Hazel and sat down beside her, speaking softly to the kitten. Once he was settled, he began to rub the top of the kitten's small head until it closed its eyes. Two more kittens meandered over, joining the sleeping kitten in Thomas's hands.

"He made the kittens sleepy," one of the girls said. Before Thomas could answer, he had five kids trying to push each other out of the way to see the kittens.

Hazel leaned in. "Alright class. Who wants to see the sleepy kittens Mr. Thomas is holding?"

Hands shot in the air.

"Line up and you can take turns petting them." Hazel pointed to a spot on the floor and the kids obediently lined up.

Thomas wasn't sure quite what to do with all the little hands coming towards him. The last time he had been around a group of children, he had been helping fill water balloons at his cousin's birthday party. That had been a few years ago.

Hazel could sense his discomfort. "If you sit still, they will take turns petting the kittens." She gave Thomas's shoulder a squeeze and then she raised her voice. "You guys are all going to be gentle, right?"

"Yes, Miss Hazel," a chorus of voices called.

Thomas glanced at Hazel, who gave him a reassuring grin.

The first girl to approach had dark brown pigtails that bounced when she scooted forward on her knees. "They are so cute," she cooed. She started to reach out her hand and then she stopped. "What if they bite me?" she asked.

"They are too sleepy to want to bite right now," Thomas said. "Even if they woke up, they don't have all their teeth yet." He pointed to the top of the calico cat's forehead. "Try petting her right here."

The little girl took another scoot forward and pressed her finger to the top of the kitten's head. "She's so soft!" she said. She jumped back with a giggle and reached for her friend's hand to pull her forward.

"One at a time," Hazel said, but the first girl was already scooting to the side so a girl with freckles across her nose could take a turn.

"Do you like kittens?" she asked Thomas, turning her button nose up so she could look him in the eye.

"I actually do," Thomas said. "I have a cat named Tiger that lives at my house."

One of the boys pushed to the front. "You have a tiger at your house?" His eyes were wide with wonder.

"No. My cat's name is Tiger." Thomas held his hand out,

showing the boy how to pet the kitten on the bridge of her nose.

"She's purring," the boy said.

Thomas glanced back at Hazel, who was gathering a couple more kittens in her hands. She dropped them on Thomas's lap, alongside the sleepy trio.

"I have to admit, this isn't what I thought we'd be doing for lunch," Thomas said. "I think I'm a fan though."

Hazel shook her head. "That's what you get when you come forty-five minutes early."

"What are you talking about?" Thomas knew he was eager to visit with Hazel, but he didn't think he'd messed up his times that badly.

"I said I'd be done at 12:30." Hazel moved to the side as the final group of kids scooted in next to Thomas.

He began to laugh. "Maybe time moves differently in vet land, but it's now 12:15 on my watch. I'm not that early."

Hazel pointed to the large clock on the wall, the hands pointing to 11:37. As she did, her eyes widened, and she held her hand over her mouth. "Oh no. The battery must have died again."

"Miss Sally? Mrs. Williams?" Hazel asked. "What time were we supposed to be done with the animal encounter?"

"Noon," Miss Sally said. She glanced at her phone and then back at Mrs. Williams, her expression mirroring the same surprise as Hazel. "Oh my gosh. We're way over time. No wonder the kittens are getting so sleepy." The parents began pulling out their own phones and shaking their heads at the time.

Mrs. Williams walked to the front of the room and clapped her hands together. "Boys and girls, it's time to say thank you to Miss Hazel and Miss Jana for letting us play."

"Thank you, Miss Hazel. Thank you, Miss Jana," the voices chorused together.

"What about him?" the little girl with pigtails asked.

"That's Mr. Thomas," shouted a little boy in the back.

"Thank you, Mr. Thomas," the voices chorused once again, before scurrying after their teachers like a herd of kittens. The parents each said thank you as they filed out behind the group.

A parakeet chirped in the corner, trying to remind the remaining adults that it was still there. Thomas looked at Hazel, the sides of his mouth twitching.

"Well, that was exhausting," Jana said. "Do you need help putting the animals away?"

Hazel shook her head. "You can head back to the front desk if you want. I'm pretty sure Thomas will help me to clean up."

"I will?" he teased.

"You will if you want your hug."

That was all the motivation Thomas needed. He gently placed the kittens in a large plastic bin that Hazel brought over. "What's the story with these guys anyhow?"

Hazel's lip jutted into a frown. "Would you believe that someone abandoned them in a box on the side of the road? I don't understand people sometimes. They could have brought them to the shelter or here, and we would have taken care of them."

"It isn't right," Thomas said.

"It really isn't. Thank goodness we had enough volunteers to help bottle feed them. Now they are getting strong enough to eat regular cat food."

Thomas could imagine the work it took coordinating the care of a litter of kittens on top of her other responsibilities. Hazel needed a break. Not more jobs to handle.

"And the kids?" he asked.

Hazel dragged her hand across her forehead. "That tour was set up weeks ago. I didn't remember they were coming until they showed up in our lobby today. It was a bonus having the kittens as part of the tour."

"It looks like you recovered well. The smiles on the kids' faces were so big!" Thomas set the last of the kittens carefully in the bin, watching as she burrowed beneath her siblings.

With the animals cleaned up, there was only one job left to do. Thomas held his arms out.

"Now, I believe I was promised a hug?"

CHAPTER 12

Hazel placed the parakeet in her cage and then straightened up, heading for Thomas's outstretched arms. He usually smelled good, but Hazel leaned into his chest, breathing deeply. She wanted to memorize every part of him now that they were dating.

"I can't believe I messed up the time so badly." Fixing the clock was getting added to her list of tasks she would get to if she ever had time.

Thomas flicked her ponytail. "Did we miss our chance for lunch?"

Her stomach growled at the thought of skipping out on food. "Oh no. We're still eating. Have you been to the sandwich shop that just opened across from the mall?"

"Not yet."

"The food is delicious, and they usually get it out quickly. Are you okay going there?"

"That sounds great." Thomas followed behind Hazel, his hand resting on the small of her back.

There were some definite perks to being a girlfriend. Hazel waited until they were outside of the clinic before she held her hand out. Thomas responded by wrapping his fingers through hers, bringing her hand to his lips for a quick kiss. It was a reminder of their unfinished business, a first kiss that was going to melt her on the spot.

The wind blew by with a chill that was unseasonably cold for the early fall days. Hazel pulled her jacket closed but Thomas was already turning her to face him. He rubbed her arm, heat trailing from where he touched. "My truck should be a little warmer than out here."

He pulled open the door and Hazel climbed in, grateful for the protection from the chilly breeze.

Ten minutes later they were sitting back in Thomas's truck, with piping hot sandwiches in a bag. After a quick check of the time, Hazel directed Thomas to her favorite park. He held the sandwiches with one hand, the bag swaying by his side, and slid his other hand around her waist.

"Where to?"

Hazel pointed to a bench perched at the top of a small hill on the other side of a large grassy field. "That table there is my favorite lunch spot."

"All the way over there?" he teased.

Hazel nodded.

"Then we might need this." Thomas reached behind the driver's seat and pulled out a folded blanket. "Today's extra cold. It feels like we're trying to skip fall entirely and start winter."

"True. It's supposed to warm back up tomorrow." As

Hazel led the way to the spot, her heart fluttered. She had a long history of moments with Thomas, but today she was sharing something new. He wouldn't understand the significance of the picnic table, but Hazel did.

It took just a minute to reach the right place. Thomas took a napkin from the bag and brushed dried leaves off the table. Then he held the food up. "Where do you usually sit?"

Hazel slid on to the bench, scooting over so there was room for Thomas to join her. He unfolded the blanket and draped it across their laps.

"Alright. Let's see if this food is as good as you said." Thomas handed Hazel her sandwich before grabbing his own.

"You're going to love it." Hazel unwrapped the end of her sandwich, wanting to keep it as insulated as possible. The first bite of her sandwich exploded on her tongue, the flavors of ham, cheese, and fresh tomatoes melding together. She sighed deeply, licking her lips.

"That good, huh?" Thomas asked. He unwrapped his own sandwich and bit down. Hazel watched with anticipation as his eyebrows shot up. He swallowed the bite, reaching for a napkin.

"Okay. That is easily the best roast beef sandwich I've ever tasted."

"I told you they were good. Do you want to try some of mine?" Hazel held her sandwich out to Thomas, taking his in exchange. They had been swapping food back and forth since they were in high school, but now Hazel could study his face while he tried something new. Her heart lifted at the smile that spread across his face.

"Remind me how you found this place," Thomas said.

"I treated the owner's dog for ticks. He gave me a free sandwich as a thank you." Hazel pushed the hair back that was tickling her face. "Although by this point, I've spent more than my fair share of money over there. It helps that it is so close to the clinic."

"And that the food is delicious." Thomas took another bite and juice dribbled down his chin.

"It really is." Hazel slid closer to Thomas so she could rest her head on his arm. "Do you know why I love coming to this park?"

Thomas pulled her closer, wrapping his arm around her shoulders so she could nestle in. "Because no one is around? I figure you liked the quiet."

He was right. There was one small playground at the end of the field that was usually empty, and the fields didn't fill until after the kids were out of school, but that wasn't the reason she liked it.

"This is where we used to come watch Danny play soccer."

Thomas pressed a kiss to the top of her head. "I remember watching him run around the field. Do you remember the year he and Bree were on the same team?"

"Weren't they like four or five?"

Thomas grinned. "Something like that. All I remember is that Danny took the ball from Bree, and she was so mad, she pushed him down."

"Oh yeah." Hazel was laughing at the memory. "She got kicked off the field for that."

"And then a half hour later she and Danny were sharing ice cream cones."

"He was always so quick to forgive." Hazel had loved that about her brother. Her heart twinged, a familiar pain that had dulled over the years, but was always present. "I can't believe he'd be a junior this year."

Thomas pulled her closer, as if his arms could hug away her pain. "I know that he was a good friend to Bree. I would have liked watching him grow up with her."

The wind blowing against Hazel's face stung the tears that pricked the corner of her eyes. "Me too. Do you remember when life used to feel easy? I mean, I know when I was in high school, I thought the world was going to be amazing. Bree reminds me of that time. All she has to worry about is her homecoming dress and which guy she will go to the dance with. I know she's had her share of hard trials, but they don't seem to weigh her down."

"Yeah." Thomas looked over the field. "Maybe it makes a difference how old you are when you experience the trials. Bree barely remembers our dad, but I do. I know there are days I still wish I could ask my dad for help. He always knew the right thing to say."

"I wish you had that too." Hazel closed her eyes, letting her heart be in the moment with Thomas. They had talked about loss before, but not with his arms wrapped around her body. His touch was comforting in a way that words hadn't been.

A question swirled through Hazel's mind. Why? Why

hadn't either of them been brave enough to take their relationship to the next level? Why had it taken them so long to admit their feelings for each other?

Hazel tried to remember a time when Thomas hadn't been in her life, but she couldn't. "Do you know that I've known you for over half of my life?"

"That makes us sound old." Thomas bumped her knee with his. "Besides, I don't count the time we knew each other in junior high."

"Why not?"

His laughter was easy. "Two reasons. Number one, my mullet. Do you remember that haircut? It was awful."

"It was all the rage. You were just being trendy." Hazel didn't tell him that he looked like a clown with his ears sticking out.

"You're being nice. My face was not made for that haircut, and I have the pictures to prove it."

Hazel covered her mouth so she wouldn't laugh out loud, but it didn't help. "Okay, okay. I'll admit it wasn't your best look. You said you had two reasons. What's the second one?"

Thomas ran his fingers through her hair. "The second reason is that we weren't friends. Back then, I was way too shy to talk to someone popular like you. You were a ten on my scale, and I didn't know how to even say hi."

"That's not true. I was just as awkward as you were in junior high. In fact, I was probably more awkward. At least you had football."

"Which lasted all of one year. I'm good at tackling livestock. Not other humans."

"Did you know that I was at your first football game, cheering you on? Even back then, I maybe had a tiny crush on you."

Thomas's shoulders shook with laughter. "Not possible. I'd have noticed you."

"Nope. I didn't tell anyone about my crush. Not even Steph. But it was there."

Thomas kissed the top of her head again. "We wasted so much time, didn't we?"

"Yeah. At least we're starting now."

"Can we make a promise now to talk about everything? Even the hard things?" Thomas rubbed his hand across her shoulders. "I don't want to lose any more time with you."

Hazel nodded. "I agree. I have spent far too many days not cuddling with you, and that is completely unacceptable."

"You know, I think you're right about that cuddling thing."

The shrill blare of Hazel's alarm interrupted the conversation. Hazel slumped her shoulders before turning it off.

"I guess that means our fun is over?" Thomas asked.

"Yep. Darn responsibilities." Hazel began to gather their trash, slipping it into the restaurant bag. She looked up, a realization washing over her. "This counts as our first official date, right?"

"I mean, I guess. Unless you want to count our time at the fair with Stuart?"

Hazel smacked his shoulder. "As fun as that was, especially with you landing in the hospital, I think I'd rather count this."

He reached for her hand, spinning her in a quick circle before he wrapped the blanket around her shoulders. "Me too. How about we call this our practice date. I'd like my first official date with you to be something we planned."

"Agreed." Hazel's feet were light when she walked back to the car, hand in hand with her favorite person. She had a long day of clients left to see, but somehow, she imagined the time would fly by.

It took just a minute to fold the blanket when they reached the car, but Hazel missed the warmth. She climbed into the cab and jabbed at the heater buttons.

"Thanks for introducing me to a new shop," Thomas said. He backed the truck out of the parking lot and turned on the road that went to the clinic.

"I'm so glad we got our practice date, even though I messed up the timing of it."

"Me too, although I really did enjoy seeing you in your element. You were great with the kids." Thomas glanced her way.

"Me? You were the one who was great with them. The kids loved you."

He reached for her hand at a stoplight, rubbing circles on the back of it with his thumb. "Are you going to make it through the rest of work, or do you need a nap after your extra-long play date?"

"Hey. I was doing those parents a favor. I may not be getting a nap, but I'm sure most of those kids will."

Thomas grinned. "I'm pretty sure my kids will wear me

out. I'll be tempted to nap at the same time." He continued to rub circles on Hazel's hand. "Have you ever thought about kids? I mean, like how many you'd like to have?"

Thomas was asking the question like a casual friend would, but daggers hit Hazel right in the heart. Most women dreamed of being a mother, but not Hazel. She wouldn't be able to save lives like she did if she was constantly worrying about her own family.

"I don't know if I want to have kids." She said the words and then glanced at the face of the cowboy from the giant family. They had been dating for less than a day, and already she could see a potentially huge wedge in their relationship. He came from a large family. It would make sense that he'd want a big family, too.

"Why would you say that?" Thomas asked. "I thought that was what all women dreamed of."

Hazel's stomach clenched and she pulled her hand away. "There's not a law that says every woman needs to have a big family. We can't all be your mom."

Thomas flinched. "I wasn't accusing you of anything. Did I say you had to have a bunch of kids?"

"No." Hazel leaned her head against the seat, her emotions swirling. She was picking a fight with Thomas about something that seemed so stupid, except she knew the question about starting a family would become important if they kept dating. It was better to address it before she fell too far in love. The problem was that Hazel was already sunk. She had tasted what a relationship with Thomas felt like, and she wasn't ready to let that go.

Thomas pulled into a parking spot, turning the engine

off. He reached for Hazel's hand, but she opened the door, climbing out before she said something she'd regret.

She slammed the door shut, but Thomas was out of the truck a second later, jogging to keep up with her.

He stepped in front of her right before she reached the clinic doors. "Will you hold on for a minute?"

Anger flashed through Hazel. Why couldn't he leave her alone so she could figure out her thoughts? "I have to get back to work."

Thomas held his hands out. "Will you please tell me why you are upset?"

"It's nothing."

"You promised we'd talk about things," Thomas said. His voice was rough with emotion, but it wasn't enough to keep her there.

Hazel swiped at the moisture in her eyes. It was stupid to be tearing up at a simple question, but in less than twenty-four hours, Hazel had found the thing that could tear them apart.

"Sometimes we make promises we can't keep." She wanted to explain her feelings to Thomas, but she didn't have the words. She wasn't ready to break apart the relationship that had barely begun.

Thomas lowered his hands and stepped to the side. Hazel pushed past him and went inside, heading straight to her office where she could shut the door and have a good cry. So much for dating the perfect man. She should have known it was too good to last.

CHAPTER 13

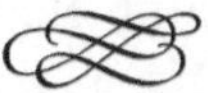

Thomas couldn't find the handbook for interpreting the female language. He wasn't quite sure where things had gone wrong. One minute he was having a great lunch with Hazel. The next, he was being shut out.

He started to drive home but realized quickly that his house was the last place he wanted to be. Porter would be able to read in his face that he was upset, and he'd want to help, but Thomas didn't know what he'd say. What he needed was a woman's perspective from someone other than his mom. She could probably be objective, but he wasn't sure.

Thomas drove until he came to the far edge of the property. That way he could check on the cattle while making his call. He walked until he found a good spot to see the cows. Then he video called his sister, Hope.

Her face lit up when she answered the phone. "Hey, big brother. How are you feeling?"

Seeing her face lifted a weight off his chest. He had forgotten how much he appreciated her advice. "I'm healing, but I have to take things slow. Do you know how annoying that is?"

His sister laughed. "I'm sorry I couldn't come to help. My professors seem to think that college is more important than visiting my wounded brother in the hospital." Hope's dark wavy hair was whipping around her face.

"Where are you?" Thomas asked.

She flipped the camera and panned over a meadow surrounded by trees that danced back and forth in the wind. Thomas could see a couple of figures walking in the distance.

"I like to come here with my friends when the city life gets to be too much. It reminds me of home."

Thomas flipped his own camera to show Hope his view. "I can see why. We're almost twins, but it isn't windy here."

Hope's face came back to the screen. "How are my cows?"

"I figured you'd ask that." He panned the camera over to a knoll where the cows were grazing. "Apart from a few run-ins with the fence, they are behaving well."

"Aw, I miss them."

Thomas grimaced. "And I miss having you around to help take care of them. Especially now that I'm out of commission."

"Do you need me to come home? I can talk to my professors again."

Thomas was worrying his sister, which was the opposite of what he wanted to do. "I definitely don't want you to do that. I'll be back to normal in just a couple more days. Right now, the Stringhams have been helping out."

"That's sweet." Hope smiled. "I'm glad people are taking care of you."

"Me too. I hate having to ask for help, but it's good to know we have it when we need it." Thomas walked over to a fence and sat down against the post. "Hey Hope? Can I get your advice on something?"

"For sure. Give me a sec to get settled." Her phone swung wildly as she climbed up on what looked like a big rock. Then the screen steadied. "I'm ready. What's up?"

Thomas looked at the sky, trying to gather his thoughts. "Well, for starters, I kind of started dating Hazel."

"You what?" Hope's eyes lit up. "When did this happen and why didn't I hear about it sooner?"

Thomas sighed. "I think it started in the hospital, but we made it official last night."

Hope cheered. "It's about time. I've been wanting you guys to get together forever."

Her enthusiasm felt like daggers, each one stabbing into his chest. "Well, don't get too excited. I may have already ruined things."

"In less than a day?" Hope frowned. "That's a pretty impressive record for screwing things up."

"You don't have to tell me that." Thomas took a deep breath. "The problem is, I don't know how to fix what I did. In fact, I'm not even quite sure what I did."

Hope brushed her hair out of her eyes. "Why don't you tell me what happened, and I'll see if I can help."

Thomas leaned his head against the post. This was why

he had called Hope. She was one of the best listeners in the family.

"We had our first kind of official date today." Thomas waited for Hope to interrupt or ask for details, but she simply nodded.

"I thought things were going great. We talked about our younger years and how much time we had wasted by waiting so long to date."

"It sounds like you guys had a good conversation. What went wrong?"

Thomas tried to remember every detail. "On our drive home, I said something about having kids. That's when Hazel froze up."

Hope shook her head. "Did you ask her how many kids she wanted to have?"

"Maybe."

"Thomas, that isn't material for first date conversations."

He rubbed the top of his head. "I mean, it's our first official date, but we've been friends for years. We've talked about a ton of serious stuff before."

"Yeah, but that was a conversation between friends. Everything you talked about was hypothetical. My guess is that your conversation today felt a little too real for Hazel. Maybe she wasn't ready for it."

Thomas shrugged. "She said she didn't want kids anyway."

Hope nodded slowly. "Oh, really? And what did you say?"

"I said I thought every woman's dream was to have kids."

Hope began to laugh. "Poor Thomas. You really stepped in it."

"By saying women want kids? I don't get it."

"No." Hope steadied the camera and looked straight into Thomas's eyes. "You assumed that Hazel was like all the other women you know. You basically implied that something is inherently wrong with her if she doesn't want to have a family."

"But I didn't say that."

"You didn't have to, at least not directly. I'm guessing that's what Hazel heard though."

Thomas looked at the sky where the clouds lazily wafted across. He tried to understand what Hope was saying, but she wasn't making sense. "Okay. So Hazel heard something I didn't say. Or she thought she heard it? I'm confused."

Hope smiled. "Hazel has been old enough to start a family for a while. My guess is she probably has people bothering her about it, and it's a sensitive subject."

That registered a little better in Thomas's brain. "What do I do? I'd hate for our relationship to be over when it's barely begun."

"That's a harder question. I think for starters, you need to apologize."

"But I didn't say anything wrong on purpose."

"I know. You didn't hurt her on purpose, but something you said made her upset. You can sit around, playing a game of who is right, or you can try to get to the root of what's really bothering her."

Hope glanced away from the phone and then back at Thomas. "My friends are calling me. I guess we have to leave. You've got this though. Just try to listen more than you talk. Let Hazel tell you what is really on her mind. You might be surprised."

Thomas cracked his neck from side to side. "Thanks, Hope. I knew you'd have the best perspective."

"That's what happens when I'm your favorite sister." She winked at Thomas. "Give Bree a hug for me and tell the rest of the family hi."

"Will do. Love you, sis."

"Love you too."

Hope ended the call and Thomas held his phone, staring at the blank screen. He had been smart to call Hope. If making up with Hazel meant apologizing, he'd say he was sorry a million times over. He just wanted to make things right.

Thomas waited to call Hazel until after dinner. He had already monopolized part of her day, and he didn't want to be a nuisance while she was at work.

She sent his call straight to voicemail which meant she was either mad at him or in the middle of treating a patient. Thomas hung up without leaving a message. She'd call back when she was ready.

Thomas had spent the night tossing and turning, waking up every few hours because his mind wouldn't stop racing. He desperately wanted to talk to Hazel before their friendship was gone.

It was early in the morning when he called her again, but he knew Hazel would be awake. She answered the call on the final ring, right before sending it to voicemail. "Hi Thomas."

He missed the warmth that usually surrounded his name. "Can we talk?"

Hazel sighed. "Look. I know there are a lot of things that we should talk about, but I can't. I'm heading out for a delivery."

Thomas could feel his moment to make things right slipping through his fingers. "Can I come?" It was his last day of work restrictions so there was nowhere else he had to be.

"To the delivery?" Hazel sounded skeptical.

"Yeah." Thomas held his breath, waiting for Hazel to give him a chance.

She sighed again. "I'll pick you up in fifteen minutes." The phone clicked off and Thomas was left holding his cell, his heart beating fast.

Fifteen minutes wasn't a long time, but it was enough time to change into a t-shirt from one of the concerts they went to after college. It was time to remind Hazel that Thomas was her friend, and someone worth fighting for.

He knew she didn't need help with the actual delivery. That's what the ranchers were for. He knew from his own livestock that it helped to have someone familiar with the animals nearby. If his job was a casual observer, he needed to make sure he took advantage of every moment he could on the drive there.

Hazel pulled up a couple of minutes early, but Thomas

was ready. He climbed into the truck, feeling the weight of a thousand unanswered questions pressing down on him.

"How was the rest of your day, yesterday?" he asked, fishing for anything to say.

Hazel's hands tightened on the wheel. "Thomas, the drive to the Bledsoe farm isn't a long one. I don't want to waste it on idle chit chat. Do you?"

Thomas shifted in the seat, turning his head towards Hazel. Her hair was pulled back into a ponytail with a few strands escaping. He wanted to brush the hair off her face, but it felt too intimate. He had one chance to make things right.

"I messed up," he said. "I don't totally understand what I did to hurt you, but it doesn't matter. The problem is that I hurt you, and I can't take that back."

"But you don't know what you did?" Hazel flipped on her blinker, turning down a two-lane road.

Thomas twisted his hands in his lap. "I know I made some assumptions about you wanting to have a family, and I probably said things in the worst possible way. I know my words hurt you. I just don't completely understand why. I was hoping you could tell me that."

He held his breath. The way he saw it, Hazel could dump him on the side of the road, or she could open up to him.

Hazel glanced his way, her eyes serious. "Thomas, your words scared me. They reminded me what different worlds we come from. Maybe there is a reason why we haven't dated before. Are we too blind to see it?"

Her words doused his thoughts, washing away any

flickers of hope. Thomas pressed his head against the window, watching the trees rush by. He needed a way to fix the relationship. Not a reason to doubt it.

"Does it matter that we're from different worlds? I think our differences are part of what makes the relationship exciting."

"Or they are the things that will rip us apart." Hazel turned down a narrow road where tree branches scraped against the side of the car. They were getting close to the ranch, and with that, their chance for conversion was ebbing away.

Thomas stretched his hand out, wanting to rest it on Hazel's arm, but he didn't know if he should. He pulled his hand back. "I want this to work."

Hazel reached up to swipe at a tear that was rolling down her cheek. "Thomas, my parents wanted things to work, too. You were at my house plenty of times when they were fighting. They started their relationship by ignoring the big issues. Eventually, the big issues splintered into enough small issues that their marriage fell apart. They didn't have a strong foundation to start with, so when the disagreements came up, there was nowhere to fall back on. You know the rest of the story. I didn't get to be raised by a mom because my parents couldn't work things out."

The emotion in Hazel's voice was pounding against Thomas's heart. He had wanted to talk to her so they could resolve things, but everything was getting worse.

"I hear what you are saying, but don't we already have a strong foundation to fall back on?" Thomas reached for

Hazel's hand. "We may not agree on every aspect of life. There are some big discussions that we still need to have. Look at our friendship though. Look what we've survived together."

"Like Danny's accident." Her voice was soft.

"And my dad's death."

"My mom leaving."

"A few too many injuries to count."

Hazel was beginning to smile through her tears.

Thomas curled his fingers around her hand, rubbing his thumb against her soft skin. "It isn't like we've spent the years flitting in and out of each other's lives on occasion. We've navigated too many hard things already. We may have a lot to explore, but I don't think communication should be one of our problems. I believe we can talk through any situation and find some sort of a compromise."

"Maybe you're right." Hazel turned on the blinker before turning onto a dirt driveway.

A small farmhouse stood at the end of the lane, with Mr. Bledsoe standing in front. Thomas had just a few seconds left to say what was on his mind.

"Will you accept my apology and give me a chance to see where this relationship can actually take us?"

The smile that Hazel gave Thomas filled him with hope. "I'd like that a lot."

CHAPTER 14

Thomas leaned against the side of the barn, watching Hazel work. She had helped with various situations on his own ranch over the years, but now he was watching her through the lens of a boyfriend. She was amazing, from the way she calmed Mr. Bledsoe's concerns to the way she quickly assessed the situation and took control.

The foal came quickly once Hazel got her into the proper position. Thomas had helped with his fair share of births on the ranch, but he still marveled that any of the animals survived the ordeal. It was amazing to watch the animals take their first breath of life.

Hazel was completely focused while she worked, but that didn't stop her from glancing Thomas's way to give him an occasional smile. Watching her move was like watching an intricate dance, from the way she calmed the horse to the way she taught the rancher how to avoid the potentially dangerous situations in the future. He could see why her services were called on so often.

His nerves didn't kick in until the delivery was over and they were both sitting back in the truck. Now there were unspoken words hanging in the air, and Thomas wasn't sure what to do with them. He wanted to pull Hazel close and kiss every inch of her face, but that felt a few steps off from where their relationship was. First, he had to make sure that he was actually forgiven.

"You were amazing back there," Thomas said. He needed something to break the silence between them.

Hazel's face softened. "That foal was so cute. Her markings will be gorgeous when she is fully grown."

Thomas nodded. "So, where to? Do you want to grab breakfast on the way home?" He was pretty sure she'd be hungry after the job.

"Not really."

His stomach sank. Had he misunderstood Hazel when she said she was ready to forgive him?

"Can I show you something instead?" Hazel's eyes gleamed with mischief.

"You're the driver." He had always admired Hazel's spontaneity. Work was demanding, yet she had more fun than most people he knew.

Hazel hummed while she drove, turning down roads that Thomas didn't recognize. He didn't start to get curious until she pulled off the side road onto a dirt road, slowly coaxing her truck around deep potholes. It was the kind of road that was meant for smaller ATVs. Not large trucks.

The motion was making Thomas slightly sick, but he

gripped the side of the seat and concentrated on the trees that whipped by with an occasional smack against the window.

"I forgot you get carsick," Hazel said. She gave his knee a little squeeze before grabbing onto the steering wheel again. "We're almost there."

Thomas groaned and rolled down his window. The fresh air helped a little bit, even if it meant dodging the occasional branch that smacked a little too close for comfort. He silently prayed that they'd be there before the nausea completely set in.

Moments after he finished his prayer, the road opened into a large clearing. Hazel slowed the truck to a stop. "We're here."

"At a field?" Thomas leaned on the edge of the window, taking in deep breaths of the crisp air to calm his body.

"It's a special field," Hazel said. She got out of the truck and walked over to Thomas's side, reaching for the door handle. "Are you ready?" Hazel pulled out her ponytail, shaking her hair loose so it caught the light of the sun.

"I think so," Thomas said. He climbed out of the truck, feeling exhausted as though he'd already run a marathon. Hanging out with Hazel was supposed to be relaxing, but he was pushing his body a little further than the doctor would probably allow. There was a reason he was supposed to take it easy for one more day.

"It's just a short walk from here," Hazel said. She reached for Thomas's hand, and his heart soared. This felt like she had forgiven him. Not for the first time, Thomas wondered why they hadn't been holding hands for years. It felt like they should always be connected.

Hazel pulled Thomas to the crest of the hill. The entire backside dropped off to reveal a lake with a small, rocky shoreline down below. Blue water stretched as far as the eye could see.

"How did I not know this was here?"

Hazel smiled. "You know this water. It's part of Farrow Lake."

Thomas tried to study the far end of the water. "There isn't any access to the back side of the lake . . ." He trailed off. "Except I guess there is. How on earth did you find this?"

There was a faint trail through the grass that led to the water's edge. He followed behind Hazel, watching her hair bounce against her shoulders as she walked towards the shore.

"I got lost one afternoon coming home from an appointment. I had helped a farmer put his horse down and I was really upset. Getting lost was the final straw for my emotions. I followed the road, looking for anywhere I could turn the truck around. When I pulled into this clearing, I got out. I was walking around to clear my head so I could handle navigating those potholes again. That's when I found the water."

She reached for his hand. When they reached the edge, she pointed to a large, flat rock which jutted out over the water. "That is my thinking spot."

The rock had large trees growing next to it, making it

impossible to see from higher on the hill. Thomas was impressed that Hazel had found it at all.

"It's in the water though." Thomas had long legs, but even he wouldn't be able to step to the rock without getting wet.

"You have to take off your boots to get there, but the water is pretty shallow." She reached down, pulling off her boots and tossing them to the side. Then she looked at Thomas, challenging him to do the same.

"Are you crazy? That water has to be freezing this time of day."

Hazel smirked. "If we were at the beach in Northern California, would you wade into the ocean?"

Thomas laughed. "Okay. Maybe. But that's the ocean. You have to get your toes wet, even if it's cold."

"Exactly. Just pretend like it's the ocean. The sun has been warming up this side of the lake for a couple of hours now."

Thomas took a steadying breath. "Give me a second." He straightened his shoulders with a deep huff and then he bent down to slip out of his boots, pulling off his socks afterwards. It took just a second to roll up the cuffs of his jeans. Then he reached for Hazel's hand. "Lead the way."

Hazel pulled him after her into the cold water, giggling when Thomas yelped. He sucked in his breath, recoiling against the chill, but it didn't last long. The heat of Hazel's hand shot through his body. He'd wade through a river full of ice if she was by his side.

Up close, the rock was larger than it had appeared from

the shore. There was plenty of room on the rock for two people to sit.

"You first," Hazel said.

Thomas sat on the rock, sliding backwards until his back was pressing against the rough bark of the tree behind him. He scooted as far to the left as he could, leaving room for Hazel to climb up.

When she settled in, there was space between them which Thomas didn't approve of. He dropped his hand to her waist, pulling her close. If heat had been rushing through his body earlier, now he was scorching next to the sun. Especially when she leaned her head against his chest.

"I like this," he said. He pressed his chin to the top of her head, breathing in a subtle scent of apple blossoms while her hair tickled against his neck.

Thomas had held Hazel in his arms before. She was an affectionate person who hugged hello and goodbye. It didn't mean anything. But now, leaning against the rough bark of the tree with his arms around her, emotions were stirring that he had been trying to keep down for years.

She rubbed a lazy circle on his arm. "I have to say, my thinking spot is a lot nicer when you're part of it. Is it strange to say that I feel safe in your arms?"

"Does that mean I'm forgiven?" Thomas trailed his hand up and down her arm. It certainly felt like she had moved past the argument.

Hazel pulled her knees up, snuggling in closer. "For now. I know we have a lot of things to discuss, but I think I'm ready to see where this adventure takes us."

"Me too." Thomas closed his eyes, letting the sun warm his face. "Remind me why we didn't try to date years ago."

Hazel shifted against his side. "I know for me, it all comes back to being afraid to ruin our friendship. Yesterday, when I thought things were over between us, I was devastated."

Thomas nodded. "Most things don't scare me, but the thought that I could be losing you yesterday terrified me, too. I can't imagine living life without you in it."

Hazel slid away from Thomas's side and swiveled her legs around, angling her body so she was facing him, with her back to the lake. The sun glanced off her hair and his heart sped up. She was beautiful.

"Here's the thing." Hazel reached out and placed a hand on his leg. "I don't have a lot of good things in my life right now. I'm so busy I can barely think, I'm worried about my dad all the time, and I don't know that I have what it takes to be in a relationship. But I'm crazy about you. As much as I worry about messing things up, I also know I can't deny what I feel."

Thomas placed his hands on Hazel's hips, scooting his body closer to hers. "I have an idea." His eyes studied every curve of her face, from the slight widow's peak on her forehead to the crinkle right above her nose. She had a spattering of dimples across her cheeks, and warm, inviting eyes. It would be easy to lean in for a kiss. Almost as easy as breathing.

Hazel's breath hitched in her throat when she answered him. "What is it?"

"What if, at least for today, we stop thinking about all

the bad things that could happen and we talk about the good things instead?"

Hazel tilted her head to the side. "That's an interesting idea." She rested her hand on his shoulder, leaning in close. "I guess, if we were in a relationship, sitting this close to you wouldn't be a problem."

He scooted another inch forward, sliding his hands from her hips to the small of her back. "Nope. Definitely not a problem."

Hazel trailed her fingers up the side of his neck, clasping them behind his head. Her touch was gentle when she began to run her fingers through his hair, but lightning shot from his scalp through the rest of his body. "A girlfriend would be allowed to play with your hair, no questions asked."

"Mmm hmm." Thomas was finding it more and more difficult to form coherent sentences. "I think that would definitely be allowed." He glanced at her lips, and then back into her eyes. They were watching him, waiting for him to make the first move.

Flirting with Hazel was fun, but he still had a chance to turn the dial back to friendship. They could get back in the truck and drive home, and things would be awkward for a day or two, but then they could keep going as friends.

He could take the easy way out. He could blame his flirtatious behavior on being tired from waking up early, and head back to the car. He could ensure that Hazel would always be in his life, but would it be enough? After worrying that he had messed up the relationship the day before, he knew he would always be wanting more.

If he leaned in just a few inches, everything would change. There was no taking back a first kiss.

That was when Thomas realized that as much as he wanted to be kissing Hazel, he wasn't sure he was brave enough. He pulled his hands back and cleared his throat, but then she parted her lips slightly. The invitation was hard to miss. This was his Hazel. If she was brave enough to cross the line, so was he.

He tilted his head down, pausing for the smallest of beats. If Hazel wanted out, she had a chance to change her mind. She lunged forward and pressed her lips to his, and he was undone. The anticipation of the kiss had been agonizing but kissing her was worth the wait. Nothing compared to the feel of her body pressing against his while his mouth danced with hers. They had tripped over the safety line their friendship offered. Now there was no going back.

Thomas leaned into the kiss, pulling Hazel closer so he could wrap his arms around her. He had wanted to talk about an escape plan that would give them an out if things moved forward too quickly, but it was too late. He sank into the kiss, shushing the warning bells that were going off in his head.

There would be time to think about caution later. All he had to worry about now was the chill of the rock beneath him, the sound of the waves crashing against the shore, and the woman sitting in front of him, whose kiss had his heart thumping erratically out of his chest.

CHAPTER 15

Hazel hadn't been sure how she'd feel when she kissed Thomas. She had thought about it more times than she cared to admit, letting her imagination get away from her, but the reality was so much better.

Her body was consumed by the moment, every nerve ending dancing. She wanted to pinch her arm to see if she was dreaming, but the rough rock scraping against her legs and the cool breeze blowing across the water felt too real to be imagined.

That meant that the strong arms wrapped around her like a blanket were also very real. Hazel sank into the kiss, trying to memorize every detail from how soft Thomas's hair was to the way his rough stubble tickled her face.

She knew that Thomas tried to be a perfectionist in everything he did, and apparently kissing was no exception. His firm kisses were impossibly tender yet strong at the same time.

Hazel's breathing was ragged when Thomas pulled

away, leaving a kiss against her forehead for good measure. She clasped her hands behind his neck, slowly moving her thumbs back and forth through his hair. His eyes flared with passion, but then a shadow crossed his face.

Hazel couldn't help but feel self-conscious. It had been a while since she kissed anyone. What if she was too out of practice? Maybe Thomas regretted it.

"What's wrong?" Hazel asked.

Thomas frowned. "I can't believe I waited this long to kiss you. What was I thinking?" He looked past her towards the lake before looking into her eyes. "Is it cheesy to say that that was awesome? Because I'm pretty sure, cheesy or not, I'd like to keep kissing you every day for the rest of my life."

"So, the kiss wasn't bad?" Hazel bit the side of her lip.

"Are you kidding?" Thomas brushed her hair back, tilting her chin up so she could look in his eyes. "Hazel Marie Wright. That was one of the best kisses of my life."

"*One* of the best?" Hazel couldn't stop smiling.

"Well, I think I need a little more research to be sure."

Hazel didn't need an invitation. She leaned forward, happy to assist with his studies. No matter where she ranked on Thomas's kiss list, he was definitely at the top of hers. Her heart was racing when she heard a splashing noise behind her.

"What on earth?" Hazel asked, pulling away from Thomas. She glanced at the water, expecting to see a fish or a bird. Instead, a kayak was rounding the corner, with a young boy paddling furiously to keep the boat upright.

Hazel jumped away from Thomas like a schoolchild

who had been caught misbehaving. She could feel the warmth rising in her cheeks as she tried to play it cool. No one was supposed to catch her kissing her best friend.

The kayaker looked up and yelled. "Hey. I need help."

Thomas whispered into Hazel's ear. "To be continued." Small shivers of excitement danced through her body as she slid off the rock into the water, right behind Thomas. The chill of the water bit into her skin the deeper she got, but it didn't matter. The only goal was to reach the boy who was paddling furiously to stay afloat.

"What's the problem?" Thomas asked, approaching the boat with his long strides.

The boy ducked his head. "My brother told me the kayak was broken, but I thought I fixed it."

As the kayak got closer, Hazel could see the problem. A large crack ran across the side of the boat, filling the bottom of the boat with water.

"My name is Thomas, and this is my friend Hazel." Thomas was close enough to grab the front of the boat. "What is your name?"

"Decker." The boy looked back and forth between Hazel and Thomas with wide gray eyes. Then he held a hand up to cover his mouth with a little gasp. "I forgot. I'm not supposed to talk to strangers."

Hazel held back a laugh. The way things stood, he wasn't in any sort of a position to be picky. She appreciated the training from his parents though.

"That is good advice to follow. When you are in trouble, it's okay to ask for help like you did." The kayak looked like it had been bleached in the sun for several years. No one had attempted any repairs because there really wasn't an easy way to fix the damage. "The crack looks bad. How did you fix it?" Hazel asked.

Decker beamed at Hazel. "I glued it together."

Hazel exchanged glances with Thomas.

"What kind of glue did you use?" Thomas asked.

"My school glue." Decker looked proud, even though his fix had clearly failed.

Thomas held on to the front of the kayak, steadying it, while Hazel reached for the oars.

"How about we tow you to shore?" she asked. "And then do you think we can call your parents?"

That caused a frown to cross Decker's face. "They are going to be really mad."

"Maybe," Thomas said. "If your mom is anything like mine, she might be a little mad but mostly she is going to be really happy that you are okay."

"Are you sure?" The boy looked at Hazel and jabbed his thumb towards Thomas. "Is he right?"

"He's right." They were close enough to the shore that Hazel could toss the oars onto dry land. "You could have gotten really hurt out there. I'm glad you wore your life jacket though. That was a good choice. Let's tell your mom where you are."

Decker held his arms up, letting Thomas lift him out of the kayak.

"Do you know your mom or dad's phone number?" Hazel asked.

"Hmm." A frown creased his forehead while he thought. "I can't remember. They got new phones. I know my mom's phone has a six in it like me. And I think there's a five."

Hazel exchanged glances with Thomas over the top of the boy's head. "What do we do?" she whispered. Her body was beginning to shiver from the cold. She had waded into the lake up to her thighs, and now a breeze was picking up.

Decker was soaked as well. His teeth began to chatter, and he grabbed Hazel's leg. "Can you just take me home?" he asked.

Thomas had water dripping off his jeans. No one was in danger of hypothermia, but Hazel knew they were all going to be really uncomfortable if they didn't move soon.

"I have an idea. Let's put your kayak in the back of my truck and then we'll figure out a plan." She reached for one end of the boat and Thomas grabbed the other. "Hey Decker, can you get the oars?"

Decker dragged the oars behind him as they walked up the hill. By the time they reached the top, he had tears in his eyes. "Water is supposed to be fun. Not cold."

Hazel knelt in front of him. "How about we take that dripping life jacket off and then you can sit in my truck? I'll turn on the heater."

He nodded and held his arms to the side. Hazel's fingers were freezing while she fumbled with the clasps.

"I've got this," Thomas said. He pressed a kiss to the top of her head. "Why don't you start the truck and get the heater going?"

Hazel met his eyes over the top of Decker's head.

Thomas was trying to hide his shivering, but she knew that he had to be freezing as well.

"I'm on it." Hazel climbed into her truck, starting the engine. She turned the heater to the highest it could go, rubbing her hands together in front of the vents. Then she knelt on the seat, reaching behind it to see if she had any blankets in the truck.

There was nothing there except for an old t-shirt that she kept for emergencies. It wasn't much, but it would give a little warmth.

Thomas opened the door and Decker climbed in. His eyes were wide as he clambered to the middle of the seat. "This truck is huge!"

"We're pretty high up from the ground." Hazel helped Thomas to buckle Decker in. Then she draped her t-shirt across his legs like a blanket.

Hazel drove slowly down the dirt road so she could avoid making Thomas car sick. He wasn't going to be able to roll down his window without freezing all of them out. His face was pale before they were half-way out.

"How are you doing?" she asked. She wanted to hold his hand, but there was a dripping child sitting between them.

Thomas pressed his hand to his stomach. "I'll be fine." He spoke through gritted teeth, which tore Hazel apart.

"Is it better if I go faster or slower?" She pushed on the accelerator and the truck lurched forward, heading right towards a giant pothole.

"Slower," Thomas moaned.

"Faster," Derek yelled.

Hazel held the truck steady, steering it around the obstacle. "Just a few more minutes," she said.

As soon as they pulled on to the main road, Thomas told her to stop. He got out of the truck and leaned against the side while Hazel looked helplessly on.

She pulled out her phone, happy to see that there were bars again. "Did you remember your mom's phone number yet?" she asked. Most kids Decker's age had their addresses and phone numbers memorized.

"I think there was a three because my little sister Linny is three. I don't know."

"Any chance you know your address?"

Decker shook his head. "My old address is 2188 E Eagle Lane, but we moved. I didn't learn the new one yet."

Hazel glanced out the window. Thomas was walking around, with the color coming back to his face. He opened the door and climbed in.

"I think I'll be okay now. Any luck calling his parents?"

Hazel shook her head.

"Maybe we should call the police," Thomas said.

Decker held both hands over his mouth. "Are they going to put me in jail?" His eyes began to well up with tears. "I was only borrowing my brother's boat. I didn't steal it."

"The police are our friends," Thomas said. "They know how to help us find houses. They aren't going to get you in trouble."

"Are you sure?" Decker asked.

Hazel nodded. "Do you know what my job is?"

He shook his head.

"I am a veterinarian. That means I help take care of animals. The police call me whenever they find an animal that needs my help. They like to help make things better."

"They'll help find my mom?"

"Yes," Thomas said. "They'll help find your mom."

Fifteen minutes later Hazel was pulling into the driveway of a modest, two-story house.

"Hey. I live here," Decker said. His face lit up. "And that's my mom."

Hazel pulled up next to the front door, watching as the woman ran down the steps towards the truck.

"Thank you so much," she said, wrapping Decker in a hug. "This all could have ended so badly."

Thomas placed a hand on her shoulder. "We were in the right place at the right time."

"You were Decker's guardian angels today. How can I ever repay you?"

"You don't need to worry about that." Hazel knelt on the ground, so she was level with Decker's face. "Will you promise me to never go on the water again unless you check with your mom first?"

Decker nodded.

She straightened up. "It was our pleasure to help."

Thomas headed to the back of the truck and pulled out the oars. "Where would you like me to put the kayak?"

Decker's mom shook her head. "You already saved my baby's life, but can I ask you another huge favor?"

"What do you need?" Thomas asked.

She stepped forward and lowered her voice to a whisper. "Please take the kayak with you. We should have thrown it away before we moved, but my older son was attached. After today, I don't think anyone wants it around. I can pay you the dump fees."

Hazel placed her hand on the woman's arm. "Don't worry about it. Why don't you take Decker inside and get him warmed up. We'll take care of the rest."

She waited until Decker was safely inside with his mom. Then Hazel climbed in the cab and looked at Thomas. "That was certainly an adventure."

"It was." He slid over so he was sitting closer to Hazel. "Would you like to go to my house and warm up?"

"Yes please."

* * *

Mom Matthews was waiting inside the door when they got to the house. She was holding a towel in one hand and a pile of clothes in the other.

"How did you know we were coming?" Hazel asked.

Thomas looked down at his phone. "I may have texted her."

"The good news is that I already have water heating up on the stove for cocoa. Why don't you two get changed and we'll see if we can get you warmed up?"

Hazel smiled, reaching for the towel. "Thank you." She followed Thomas down the hallway, turning a corner to the bathroom.

As soon as they were outside the view of Mom Matthews, Thomas pulled Hazel into a hug. "Are you okay?" he asked.

She leaned her cheek against his chest. "Apart from being soaking wet, I'm doing fine." Hazel stood on her tiptoes and gave Thomas a kiss on the cheek. "Actually, I'm pretty great. The morning didn't go how I expected, but I'm okay with that."

Thomas stroked her cheek with his hand before he stepped back. "Me too. I'll meet you in the kitchen in a few."

Hazel's heart was soaring when she closed the door behind her. She didn't know what the future held, but she was certain it held more kisses with Thomas. That was a future she could look forward to. She pulled on the dry clothing with a smile, her lips tingling in anticipation of what would come next.

CHAPTER 16

The only thing better than sitting on the couch with Hazel was snuggling on the couch, fuzzy blankets wrapping them in a nest while they sipped hot cocoa. Her body had stopped shivering a while ago, but Thomas still held her in his arms.

"How much longer until you have to go to work?" he asked.

"Ten minutes. I wish I had longer."

"Me too." Thomas set his mug on the table, turning to face her. "This may be a stupid question because I feel like I should know the answer, but are you always this busy? It feels like every time I try to do something with you, you're at work."

"It's the season. Fall and spring seasons have me busy with calving. It will calm down in a few weeks, and then I'll just have occasional emergencies to deal with."

Although Thomas admired Hazel's work ethic, he selfishly wanted her all to himself. "I guess I should probably share you, but I really don't want to."

That earned a laugh from Hazel. "I'm only on call tomorrow. We could hang out then, unless I get called in."

Thomas was tempted to cancel his plans, but he already was booked. "At the risk of repeating a bad day, I really am going back to the fair tomorrow with my family. Someone kind of ruined things by making us all go to the hospital instead."

"I guess you really did figure out how to cut that day short. I could call Stuart and see if he wants to come."

Those were fighting words. Thomas reached for the ticklish spot on Hazel's knee, causing her to roll to the edge of the couch. She picked up a throw pillow and held it in her hands, facing Thomas with a smirk.

He grabbed the pillow beside him in response. "I'm armed, too," he said. "And I have a longer reach."

Hazel smacked him with the pillow anyway. "I'm pretty sure you tickled me first. I have no mercy."

"Hey," Thomas said. He curled up in a ball to avoid the pillow that was pummeling him. "You started it by mentioning Stuart."

She paused; the pillow held high in one hand. "True."

Thomas's heart began to beat faster when Hazel put the pillow down and scooted back to his side. She kissed his cheek. "I'd love to go to the fair with you."

"This time as my official date?" Thomas wasn't going to leave any room for interpretation this time around.

"I like the sound of that. Yes. As your date."

With those words, it didn't matter to Thomas that he had one more day of light movement ahead of him. He could handle a little bit of boredom because the next time he saw Hazel, he'd be off restrictions and on a date with the woman of his dreams. The morning couldn't come soon enough.

* * *

THOMAS HADN'T SLEPT WELL, tossing and turning in anticipation of the date to come. He couldn't wait to take Hazel to the fair as his official girlfriend. It was going to make all their activities so much more fun.

He was brushing his hair to the side when Reid poked his head through the bathroom doorway.

"Porter. I found him," Reid yelled.

"Hey Reid. What's up? You guys almost ready?" Thomas straightened the collar on his shirt before giving his reflection a final nod. Porter pushed into the bathroom, his hands behind his back. "We're ready, but you're not."

"What do you mean?" Thomas studied his reflection. His shirt was buttoned properly, and he had brushed his teeth and shaved. It wasn't like this was his first time getting ready for a date. With his hair behaving exactly the way he wanted it to, he knew he looked good.

Porter nodded at Reid. "I can't believe you're trying to shirk on your responsibilities."

"Yeah," Reid chimed in. "We have rules at this house."

Thomas looked back and forth between his brothers, trying to figure out what they were talking about. Then he saw a flash of gold behind his brother's back and his stomach sank.

"You've got to be kidding me."

Porter's grin grew as he pulled out a large belt, the buckle at least four times the size of anything a normal human would wear. The bulls with the clashing horns were a good touch for an eight-year-old, but not for a grown man.

He shook his head, trying to duck out of the bathroom but Porter and Reid formed a wall. He hadn't spent much thought on the outfit he was going to wear, but he knew it didn't include a giant belt buckle with bulls on it.

"No thanks. I'm already dressed," Thomas said. He knew he was fighting a losing battle, but he was going to give his best efforts to avoid the situation.

"It's tradition," Reid said.

"Yeah. I wore it for Emily," Porter chimed in.

"But the point of the belt is to see if the girl has a sense of humor. We already know Hazel does."

"It doesn't matter. Rules are rules." Porter held the belt in his hands, his glare making Thomas squirm.

"She already knows about the belt. In fact, if you think about it, this isn't even our first official date. I already missed my window."

"I'm hearing a lot of excuses," Reid said. "Will you put the darn thing on so we can go?"

Thomas glared back and forth between his brothers. Wearing the belt was okay if it was a first date with someone you weren't sure about. If the girl bailed, no big deal. This was his Hazel though. What if, after all the years of waiting, this was the thing that made her change her mind about giving a relationship a shot?

"Do you know how hard it was to convince Hazel to finally try a date with me? I'm not messing that up."

Reid planted his hands on his hips. "So, you'd rather be late? I thought you had your honor and all."

As frustrating as it was, Reid had a point. Thomas huffed and grabbed the belt from Porter's hands. "Fine."

He fastened the buckle to his jeans, rolling his eyes before he turned to glare at Reid. "Just you wait, Reid. Your turn will come."

"It's cool. I've already worn the buckle on plenty of dates. Most women seem to dig it."

Porter clapped Reid on the shoulder. "And that is why you are still single."

The men filed out to the family room where Mom Matthews, Bree, and Emily were waiting. Emily took one look at Thomas and doubled over laughing.

"Poor Hazel," she said. "Have you really never worn the buckle for her before?"

Thomas shook his head. "We've hung out dozens of times, but never on an official date."

Bree grabbed her sweater from off the chair. "I am so glad that tradition just belongs to the men of this family. You look ridiculous."

"Thanks, sis. I couldn't agree more." Thomas pushed his way out the door to the car. It was time to get to Hazel's house so he could get his embarrassing moment over with.

His stomach was in his throat when he knocked on Hazel's front door, golden belt buckle gleaming in the sun.

He could hear a muffled "hold on" through the door. A minute later, the door swung open.

Thomas looked at Hazel, trying to take in what he was seeing. She was wearing a pale pink dress that hugged her body in all the right places to accentuate her soft curves and a pair of brown boots that went to her knees. Her hair hung down in loose curls, with the sides pulled up. Hazel didn't usually wear makeup, but this time she had on just enough to highlight her beautiful blue eyes.

He took all of this in with quick succession, landing on her finishing touch. Hanging from her ears were the largest pair of gold earrings Thomas had ever seen. A huge sheep hung from one ear, its chubby body dangling from a small flower. The other ear had a cow with a jointed tail that allowed the cow to sway back and forth.

Hazel's eyes crinkled when she saw Thomas and she pumped her fist in the air. "Yes! I was hoping you'd be dressed appropriately."

Thomas was at a loss for words. He stepped to Hazel's side, picking her up so he could spin her in a circle. Then he dipped her, placing a quick kiss on her lips. He ignored the cheering that erupted from the car.

"You're incredible," he said, grinning so wide his cheeks hurt.

"I figured you'd be wearing that silly belt, so I thought I'd match." Hazel wiggled her head slightly, causing the earrings to dance against her neck. "What do you think?"

"Where did you find those? I'd like to say they are as gaudy as the belt, but I think they are worse." Thomas reached for her hand.

A faint flush filled Hazel's cheeks. "I bought them last year on the last day of the fair."

"But I was with you at the fair. How did I miss it?"

Hazel laughed. "I had Steph distract you. Remember when she twisted her ankle, and you ran to get her some ice?"

"Yeah."

"That was fake, but it gave me enough time to buy these earrings without you noticing. I was really hoping I'd get to wear them for you one day."

Thomas hugged Hazel to his side. "Are you sure it's worth it?"

She gave his waist a squeeze. "Most definitely. So, my handsome cowboy. Are you ready to go?"

Thomas looked down at his date, taking in every detail. "How brave are you feeling?"

"What do you mean?"

"Well, my brothers forced me to wear this belt to pick you up. What do you think about wearing our accessories through the fair? I'd love to embarrass them a bit." The belt had been worn numerous times, but never for an extended period of time.

Hazel rubbed the side of his arm. "I'm game if you are."

Thomas proudly led his date to the car, opening the door for her. She slid into her seat amidst excited chatter. There was no question about whether Hazel would fit into his family. She handled their teasing like a pro. By the time they got to the fair, Hazel had convinced Bree to look for a matching pair of earrings.

They were standing in line to head into the tractor pull

arena when Mom Matthews pulled Thomas to the side. "She's perfect for you," she said.

Thomas nodded. "Thanks, Mom. She makes me happy." He reached for Hazel's hand and pulled her close.

"Do you want to come with me to grab snacks for the family?" They needed their popcorn for watching the tractors, but Thomas had an ulterior motive in mind.

He waited until they were out of sight of the bleachers. A narrow strip ran between the tents as a walkway for the vendors to use. Thomas pulled Hazel behind one of the tents.

"What are we doing?" she asked.

Thomas brought his hand up to her cheek. "I wasn't able to say hi properly before." He slid his hand behind her neck.

Their first kiss had been interrupted, but now Thomas was determined to not let another day pass without showing Hazel exactly how he felt. He pressed his lips to hers, the sounds of the fair fading to the distance.

When he straightened up, he caressed her cheek. "Hello," he said.

Hazel smoothed down the back of his hair. "Hi. I think I can get used to this greeting."

Thomas held out his hand and Hazel grabbed it. Thomas was floating when they walked out from behind the tent together. He had years of kisses to make up for, but he was making a good start.

They snuck a couple more kisses waiting in line for various snacks. By the time they got back to the tractor pull, Thomas's arms were full but so was his heart. Hazel was filling in the pieces that had been missing for so long, he had forgotten his heart could be whole.

He settled in to watch the tractor pull, sighing with happiness when Hazel slid her hand through his. The tractor pull ended with Hazel and Thomas's favorite choice winning the entire contest. They cheered along with the rest of the crowd, but Thomas's eyes were only for Hazel.

There was a small debate about where to go after the tractor pull. Bree had her heart set on seeing the animals, but Thomas and Hazel had one more tradition they had to do. Otherwise, the fair wouldn't be complete.

"Did you pick your prize yet?" Thomas asked.

"What prize are you talking about?" Bree asked.

Hazel grinned. "Thomas has been winning me prizes every year since the first year we came to the fair."

"Yeah. And each time the prize gets bigger and bigger." Thomas held his hands out, making a large circle. "I think the bunny I won for her last year was this big."

Hazel reached up to close the circle a bit smaller. "More like this. And yes. I've picked my prize."

Emily reached for Porter's hand. "This sounds like a good tradition to start. Are you in?"

Thomas grinned. "Should we up the stakes?"

"What do you mean?" Porter asked.

"The person who wins the biggest prize for their woman gets to swap chores with the loser." Thomas knew Porter wouldn't back down from the challenge.

"Hey. That's not fair. Some of us didn't bring a woman to compete for." Reid said.

Bree grabbed his arm. "We can be a team. And if I lose, I'll help you with the chores."

"Awesome." Reid folded his arms in front of his chest. "We're in."

Thomas rolled his shoulders, loosening them up for the battle. "Alright, Hazel. What prize am I winning you this year?"

CHAPTER 17

Hazel led the way to the games tent, her mind spinning. The first year Thomas had won her a small purple teddy bear holding a heart. She never told Thomas, but she kept every prize he won her year after year, lining them up on a shelf in her room. At times it seemed juvenile to be holding on to cheap fair toys, but each one represented a memory with Thomas.

This year, she'd been eying the stuffed unicorns. They weren't the biggest of the toys, but she wasn't ready to have a stuffed, four-foot-tall puppy in her room yet.

Hazel grabbed Thomas's hand, leading the way to the ring toss booth.

"You're already at a disadvantage," Thomas said, scowling at his brothers. "I'm the master of the ring toss."

"Oh really?" Reid said. He rolled up his sleeves. "I'm sure I can take you."

Porter scuffed his feet against the ground like a bull getting ready to charge. "Don't count me out."

The brothers turned as a unit to look at their mom. "You're going to be the judge, right?"

"Always." She had a smile on her face that hinted at years of breaking apart silly disputes between her boys.

Hazel walked to Emily's side. "I hope you like stuffed unicorns," she whispered, laughing as the brothers sized up the game. "I'm pretty sure we aren't leaving here until they all have won something."

Emily gave Hazel's arm a squeeze. "I think it's cute that they get along so well. They fight, but you can tell they love each other."

"That's true." Hazel had watched the brothers banter over the years. The three oldest brothers had a special bond.

"What are the rules?" Bree asked.

"I don't know about you two," Thomas said, "but I plan on winning the biggest unicorn for my lady, here."

Hazel laughed. "I want the white one with the sparkle tail."

"Alright." Thomas stepped up to the line. "First person to score enough points for the giant unicorn wins."

"And who does the chores?" Reid asked.

"Both the losers," Porter said. He ran to Emily's side. "A kiss for good luck?"

Hazel's heart jumped watching Porter and Emily together. She turned Thomas to face her. "You can't let him have all the good luck." She pressed a kiss to his cheek, self-conscious to be so affectionate in front of his family.

Bree backed away from Reid. "No way you're getting a good luck kiss from me."

"How about a fist bump?" Reid asked.

"Boom," Bree said, waving her fingers in the air after they bumped fists. "You've got this."

Thomas stepped up to the line and Hazel could barely watch. In wanting to win her unicorn, she had unwittingly set a contest in motion. If Thomas lost, he'd be doing extra work. What if his incisions hadn't healed properly? She couldn't exactly check them herself.

Instead, she put all her mental energy into cheering him on. "Yes!" she said, pumping her fist in the air as Thomas landed his first toss around the neck of a ten-point bottle.

Reid stepped up next and threw his ring, narrowly missing the fifty-point bottle.

"Close," Thomas said. "But not good enough."

Porter's toss landed on a twenty-point bottle. "That's how you do it," he said.

Hazel held her breath when Thomas threw the next ring, watching it sail through the air to fall by the side of the wall.

The score went back and forth, with brothers slapping down more and more coins to earn enough points for the main prize. Hazel had been sure Thomas would win outright since he had taken the early lead, but Reid was catching up quickly.

They were getting close to the final prize when Thomas held his hand up. "Time out," he said. "I need to consult with my team manager."

He walked over to Hazel, his eyes bright. Competition looked good on Thomas.

She held her hand out and tugged him to the side. "What's the plan?" she asked. "Porter is probably out of it, but Reid can land those high point tosses."

"Yeah, but he's not consistent. I'll win the unicorn if I land another twenty-pointer, but he'll beat me if he goes for a fifty." Thomas said.

Hazel rubbed his arm. "Consistency has been your move this whole game. You've landed more shots than Reid. I think you're good playing it safe."

Thomas stretched his tossing arm over his head. "What if he comes from behind?"

Hazel stood on her tiptoes to whisper in his ear. "Then I guess you'll have to make it up to me some other way." She kissed his cheek and stepped back.

Thomas held his hand over his cheek, a grin stretching across his face. "You're going down," he said, pointing to his brothers.

Porter stepped up first. He threw his final ring, and it landed around the thirty-point bottle.

"Here's your prize." The kid running the booth held out a small unicorn with a bow around its neck.

Hazel watched as Emily took the unicorn from Porter, her face lighting up like he had won her the greatest trea-sure of all time. They really were an adorable couple. She turned her attention back to the game. Thomas was up.

"You've got this," she said, crossing her fingers.

Thomas tossed the ring with a perfect wrist flick. It soared through the air, landing securely around the neck of the thirty-point bottle next to Porter's ring.

"That wins the top prize," the boy said from behind the stand. He reached for a unicorn, but Reid stopped him.

"I've got one more toss. My sister may want to choose a different prize when we win."

Hazel bit the side of her cheek. All Reid needed was one lucky throw to clench the prize. She walked to Thomas's side, reaching for his hand.

"Miss it, miss it, miss it," she chanted under her breath. She hated the thought of Thomas having to do the chores for his brothers. He could handle it, strength wise, but knowing the brothers, they'd probably find the stinkiest or grossest jobs to pass along.

Reid stepped up to the booth and cracked his knuckles.

Bree cheered him on. "You've got this!" She slapped him on the back and then stepped back.

Reid flicked his wrist, and the ring flew through the air, straight towards the fifty-point ring. Like Thomas predicted, he wasn't going to play it safe. Everyone held their breaths as the ring landed on the bottle's neck, swinging around it once before it flew off, landing on the ground.

Hazel threw her arms around Thomas's neck. "You did it!" She kissed his cheek before stretching her arms out to take the unicorn that the teenager at the booth was holding out.

"Nice job," Bree said. She picked out her second-place prize, a hippo wearing a top hat. "So, Thomas. What chores are you going to torture us with?"

Thomas rubbed a circle up and down Hazel's back. "I'll let you know when I think of something good."

Hazel held the unicorn to her chest. Usually, winning the prize was the last stop they made before leaving the fair, so no one was stuck lugging stuffed animals around.

Thomas was reading her mind. "Alright, folks. Who's ready to go home?"

The family headed to the car, but Thomas and Hazel lingered behind the group.

"Did you have fun?" Thomas asked.

Hazel nodded. "Yeah. I mean, you aren't exactly Stuart, but I guess it was okay." She jumped to the side to escape the tickle that was coming her way.

"I personally am happy I'm walking out from the fair instead of getting carted out on a stretcher, although I really don't remember much of that ride."

"I'm just happy that our fair streak is back intact. My shelf was looking pretty lonely without a prize to add to it."

Thomas stopped walking and Hazel realized her mistake.

"Your shelf? I'm confused."

Hazel held the unicorn up to hide her face. "There's a small chance I've kept every single prize you've ever won for me."

"Seriously?" Thomas pressed the unicorn to the side. "That's kind of adorable."

"Are you sure it isn't too cheesy? The girls make fun of me all the time."

Thomas reached for her hand and kissed it. "They just don't have your incredible tastes."

Hazel's body was floating. "You know one of my secrets. I want to hear one of yours, now."

Bree chose that moment to yell back at them. "Hurry up, you two. You're taking forever."

"We're coming," Thomas answered. He gave Hazel's hand a squeeze. "I guess you're going to have to wait to find out."

Hazel smiled. That implied that there were going to be more dates to look forward to. She was excited to see what came next.

ALL HAZEL GOT WAS a quick kiss goodbye when Thomas dropped her off at her apartment, with his family looking on. Playing at the fair had been magical, but now it was time to get back to real responsibilities.

"Can I see you tomorrow?" he asked.

"Yes, please." Hazel made sure Thomas was gone before she ran to her room with the unicorn, scooting the other toys closer together so there was room for her new addition. Her friends were going to tease her about it, but she didn't care. This unicorn came with kisses, and that was worth holding on to.

The next day Hazel couldn't stop yawning. She had spent half the night thinking about Thomas's question and what he wanted to say. Sundays were usually a day to sleep in, but Hazel was up before dawn. She grabbed a quilt and went to sit on the porch, watching the sun rise over the mountains.

It was agony waiting for Thomas to be awake. Most

people didn't appreciate early morning calls. She watched the minute hand on her clock, waiting until it hit 8:30. Then she tapped on his name, pulling up their text chain.

Good morning, sleepy head. Are you awake yet?

Yawn. I am now. What's up?

I had fun yesterday. Do I get to see you today?

Hazel held her phone, watching the dots flicker across the screen while Thomas wrote his reply. She tried to be patient, but a minute later, when he still hadn't finished his sentence, she gave up and pushed the button to call him.

"Hello?" Thomas said, making his voice gravelly.

Hazel pulled the quilt around her shoulders. "Nice try. The Thomas I know wouldn't still be sleeping."

"Did you ever think that I wore my arm out doing that ring toss? Maybe I need some extra time to wake up this morning."

"Nice try, cowboy. You didn't answer my text."

"Yes I did. I asked you if you wanted to go on a picnic today." Thomas yawned. He may not have been exaggerating about sleeping in.

Hazel checked her phone but there was no message. "It didn't send."

Thomas went quiet for a second, and then started laughing. "Sorry about that. It should be on the way now."

The phone dinged and Hazel read the message.

I'd love to see you today. How does a picnic sound? I know a perfect place.

Butterflies danced through her body. "Thanks. And yes. A picnic sounds great."

Thomas whooped. "How does 12:30 sound?"

It was four hours away, but Hazel would make do. She supposed she could entertain herself at home if she needed to.

"I can't wait." Hazel hung up the phone and pulled open her dresser drawers. She had a hallway closet to organize, but first, she had to make sure the perfect outfit was ready.

The hours crept by slowly, but as soon as Thomas knocked on the door, her body relaxed. She stepped forward, greeting him with a kiss. That was something she was happy to get used to.

He held her at arm's length. "Have I told you how beautiful you look today?"

"Not yet." Hazel raised her eyebrows. "Have I told you how handsome you look?"

Thomas kissed the top of her head. "Well, now that we've established that we both are incredibly gorgeous people, how do you feel about getting a little messy?"

"Are you expecting a food fight?" Hazel asked.

"No, but the place I want to take you is a little off the path. We may get a few leaves and branches on our jeans."

Hazel narrowed her eyes. "How far off the path? Do I need to put on hiking boots?"

"Nope. You may want a jacket though. The spot is shady."

"Yes, sir." Hazel pulled her jacket off the hook by the front door and locked the door behind her. She climbed into the cab of the truck, smiling at the pile of blankets stacked on the seat. Thomas was definitely prepared for a picnic.

"How far away is it?" Hazel asked.

"Just a few minutes."

Hazel watched with surprise as Thomas headed up Old Ranch Road. He turned down a dirt road on his property. The road curved and headed up a hill, leading to a thicket of trees.

"You're taking me home?"

Thomas pulled to a stop in the clearing right outside the trees. He turned off the engine.

"Not quite, but we are here." He opened the door and hopped out. Hazel was laughing by the time he pulled open her door.

"Does it count as a date if we haven't left your property."

"We didn't need to." Thomas held his hand out. "Are you ready?"

"What about the picnic? And the blankets? Don't we need to grab some stuff?"

He shook his head. "Not yet."

Hazel was confused when she followed behind Thomas, but she was ready for the adventure.

He led the way, holding aside branches so they didn't smack her in the face. As they walked, she began to make out the faintest signs of a pathway.

"One more minute," Thomas said. When they reached the top of the hill, he turned around, leaning down to kiss Hazel's surprised mouth.

"Remember that bet I won yesterday?"

"Yep. Did you figure out the chores you wanted your siblings to do?"

Thomas grinned and stepped to the side, waving to the clearing behind him.

A picnic was set out at the top of the hill, with blankets, fluffy throw pillows, and a wicker basket in the center of it.

"I told them they had to make us a date, and this is what they came up with."

Hazel held her hand to her mouth, turning slowly to take in the view. Tall trees ringed a small clearing, with a river running along the edge.

"It's beautiful," she said.

"Just wait until you see the surprises they've planned."

Hazel ran forward, sitting in the center of the blankets. "Should I be worried?"

Thomas sat down beside her, wrapping her in a hug. "No way. It's going to be great."

As if on cue, the sounds of violin music filled the air. Bree appeared from behind a cluster of trees, slowly playing a song that sounded half like a funeral march. She had taken violin lessons at one point, but clearly hadn't kept up with them. A moment later, Reid popped his head out of the trees. He held a trash can lid in one hand and a large stick in the other, which he used to bang out a steady rhythm to accompany Bree.

Hazel couldn't stop laughing when Porter came out from the trees holding a pair of maracas. He shook them wildly, not even trying to match his siblings. The best part of the performance was when Emily came out, her hands clasped in front of her while she began to sing. She was a woman of many talents, but singing was not one of them.

The makeshift band marched up to the side of the picnic bench and stopped playing. Porter pulled out a paper that had been stuffed in his pocket and began to read with a loud voice.

"Hear ye, hear ye. This is the official picnic site of Thomas Donavan Matthews and Hazel." He looked at Hazel with panic in his eyes. "What's your middle name?" he asked.

"Marie," she whispered.

"Ahem. This is the official picnic site of Thomas Donovan Matthews and Hazel Marie Wright. Should you require any assistance, blow this whistle and we will be at your service."

Reid dropped to one knee, holding out a tray with a pink plastic whistle in the center of it.

"For now, enjoy the delectable offerings of our mother."

Bree poked Porter in the side.

"I mean, enjoy the delectable offerings of Lady Matthews."

Hazel leaned against Thomas's side, trying to keep a straight face.

"Thank you, kind sirs and madams," Hazel said. "I think we are fine for now."

"Then we will leave you to your food," Emily said.

"Enjoy," Bree called. She lifted her violin to her chin and the ensemble followed behind, playing an off-key song while they left the clearing.

Hazel opened the picnic basket, her heart full of laughter. It didn't matter what food Mom Matthews had made.

Hazel had eaten enough of her cooking to know that it would be delicious. She could be served dry toast and she'd probably still be grinning ear to ear because she was sitting next to the man of her dreams. Life couldn't get any better than that.

CHAPTER 18

Two weeks had passed since the picnic, and Thomas hadn't stopped grinning whenever he thought about how well his life was going. He was back to full strength, which meant his days were busy working on the ranch, helping to prepare for the snowy winter that was coming before too long.

The highlight of every day was finishing up with whatever task he had been working on and then meeting Hazel. Sometimes he went to her vet clinic, bringing her a bagel or a treat to help her get through a long evening of on-call work. Other times she came to the ranch, snuggling on the couch while they watched movies with his family.

It didn't really matter what the activity was, as long as it involved Hazel. Thomas was rotating the feed bags when Steph called.

"What's up?" Thomas asked, turning the speaker on so he could set his phone on a shelf.

"It's Hazel's birthday in two weeks," she said.

"I know. I've been trying to figure out the perfect gift to buy her. I still have to figure out our activity, too." Thomas had been friends long enough to know that missing Hazel's birthday would be worse than missing Valentine's Day. She usually celebrated the entire month of her birthday instead of just one day.

"I think I can help with the activity part of things. I made reservations for six at Cocoa Castle a few months ago. Hazel has been talking about going there ever since they did the tv special on the chocolate lava cake."

Thomas picked up his phone, leaning against the barn wall. "You're saying I can't see her on her birthday? That doesn't seem right."

"Not at all. There's room for you to come." Steph yelled at her dog to stop barking. Then she was back. "I was actually hoping you'd help us surprise her. We didn't tell her about the reservations."

That was a job Thomas was happy to do. He said goodbye to Steph and got back to work, planning out what he could say. Hazel wouldn't see the party coming.

Finding a diversion for Hazel's party was proving to be more difficult than Thomas expected. He asked her to save her some time on her birthday, but she shrugged it off, saying it wasn't a big deal and he didn't need to bother. That wasn't the Hazel that Thomas knew.

"Do you have a secret boyfriend that I don't know about?" he teased when she turned him down for the third time. "And you made plans with him?"

She shrugged, lifting her hands into the air. "I can't tell you everything about me. Where's the mystery in that?"

Thomas didn't bring up birthday plans again until the following day. "We could go see a movie or get dinner somewhere."

"No thanks. I'm good." Hazel turned her attention to the bandages in front of her, rolling them tightly before placing them in a storage bin.

Thomas waited until his drive home to call Steph back. "I think she suspects something," he said.

"No way. I've kept it a total secret."

"Are you sure? Because she keeps shutting me down whenever I ask her out."

"Huh. That's strange. She usually loves her birthday."

"Exactly. That's why I think she knows something is up." Thomas ran a hand through his hair, trying to keep his cool. Steph wasn't listening to him. She was convinced she was right about Hazel.

"Keep trying," she said.

"I will." Thomas wasn't used to working with Steph, but he did want the day to be special for his girlfriend. If that included a surprise dinner, that was fine with him.

Thomas was brushing down the horses later that day when Hazel called him.

"Hi, my love," he said. "Why won't you let me spoil you for your special day?

"It's just another day on the calendar. It's not a big deal."

Thomas snorted. "Since when?" He had been writing Hazel's birthday on his calendar for years.

Hazel was quiet. Then she sniffed. "Since I'm turning thirty."

"And?" Thomas stopped brushing Bella's mane and gave her a pat. Hazel had never been shy about her age before.

"Nothing," Hazel said. "How was your ride?"

She was avoiding the subject and Thomas was determined to figure out why.

"I'm going to leave the day open for you on your birthday. As for my ride, it was beautiful. I'd love to take you to see the fall leaves before they drop."

"That would be fun," Hazel said.

The conversation moved to other things and Thomas let the subject of her birthday go, but now he had a mystery to unfold

Four days later Hazel was still dodging the question. Thomas had moved from a simple curiosity to an all-consuming desire to know why she was behaving so out of character.

It wasn't until he was heading into the care center with Hazel that he realized what the problem was. He watched her interact with her dad, and by the time they left, his suspicions were confirmed.

"He doesn't know your birthday is coming up, does he?"

Hazel shook her head. "He doesn't even know who I am. Why would he remember my birthday?"

The emotion in Hazel's voice was breaking Thomas's heart. Especially when a flicker of a memory crossed his mind. "This is a decade birthday, and your dad did something extra special for your tenth and twentieth birthdays, right?"

The tear rolling down her cheek told him he was on the right track.

"It's just a silly tradition," Hazel said. "We were supposed to have a lot more of them together."

Thomas wrapped his arms around her, pulling close. "I can't begin to understand what it would feel like to have one of the people who loved you most in the world not remember you anymore. I could tell you that your dad still loves you, because deep down inside I am sure he does, but that doesn't help with the present."

"He thought I was his housekeeper today. I guess someone with blonde hair cleans his room twice a week, and that's who he figured I was." The carefully crafted mask on Hazel's face had slipped, letting Thomas see more of her pain.

"Which means no birthday celebrations for sure." Thomas didn't know what else to say. A special birthday celebration would feel meaningless when all she wanted was her dad to notice her. That was when the idea began to percolate.

Thomas called Steph that evening. "We need a new birthday plan," he said.

"What are you talking about? My plan is perfect."

"It would be, except this is a decade birthday." Thomas waited for the reaction he knew would come.

"That's the point. I want it to be a big celebration . . ." Steph trailed off. "Oh. Right. I can't believe I didn't make the connection. Poor Hazel."

"Yeah. She was pretty sad earlier today. I don't know how to help her." Thomas was standing next to the horse barn. He leaned against the warm wood, lifting a booted foot to rest it on the wall behind him. Fixing things was something he was usually good at. He had an idea, but it wasn't fully formed. Steph was honest enough she would tell him if it was stupid or not.

"What if we had a party at the residential care facility where her dad is committed?" Thomas asked. "It would let her be with him on her special day."

Steph hummed before she spoke. "What if it backfires? He won't recognize her, which could make everything much worse."

"True," Thomas said. "Let's simmer on it and see what we come up with. There has to be something we can do to make it special for her."

"I agree," Steph said.

THOMAS STILL HADN'T COME up with any better ideas and Hazel's birthday was just a week away. Nothing he thought of felt good enough. Hazel kept assuring him that she was happy to sit that birthday out and let it be a quiet one, but Thomas didn't believe her. He had seen too many years of her making such a big deal about her birthday, that everyone in town seemed to remember it. Even the local bakery sold special hazelnut cupcakes the entire month of October as a nod to Hazel.

He was desperate for an idea, but inspiration didn't strike until Thomas was mucking out the chicken coop. The manure would make a great fertilizer for the garden the following year but getting it over to the compost heap was tedious. The shovel was scraping along the boards when Thomas remembered an old picture from one of his mom's parties.

Each of the guests was dressed in costume, ranging from a gardener holding a head of lettuce to a woman draped in jewels. It was a murder mystery party, and everyone had a role to play.

He called the care facility to see if they could use the cafeteria for a last-minute celebration. Then he called Hazel.

"Look. I know this year is a difficult one with your dad not remembering you. What if we bring the party to him? We could have a costume party. If everyone dresses up, he won't recognize anyone. Maybe it will take a little bit of the sting away." Thomas hoped he was on the right track towards helping Hazel, and not making everything worse.

"I don't understand how that would make things better."

"It won't. Nothing can make things better for you, but you'll be able to spend some time with him on your special day." He crossed his fingers, willing Hazel to agree to the idea.

"Is it okay if I think about it?"

"For sure, but don't take too long. Your birthday is coming up soon."

"Ugh. Don't remind me." A half hour later Hazel called back. "I'm in."

Thomas flung the shovel into the shed, cringing when it crashed against the other tools, toppling half the other tools to the ground. Bree would fuss at him, but he'd take care of the tools later. He had less than a week to pull together a party for Hazel that would help ease some of the sadness on her heart. Thankfully, he knew who to call for help.

Thomas and Steph managed to notify all of Hazel's friends about the event before the day was through. Each person got an assignment to bring a snack, so the food was taken care of. Porter and Emily volunteered to do the decorations. Some of their ideas were awful but Thomas didn't care. He crossed his fingers that everything would be perfect in the end.

On the day of Hazel's party Porter and Emily brought their decorations to the care center. They worked side by side, laughing whenever a balloon popped. They weren't a professional decorating crew, but they brought the spirit of fun. Thomas was grateful for their help.

They finished decorating ten minutes before Hazel's party was ready to start. Her party looked like a cross between a birthday party and a harvest dance. Pink balloons were mixed with orange jack-o-lantern faces, and the smell of roasted hot dogs competed with the aroma of fresh baked cookies.

Thomas paused in the doorway for a final inspection, laughing at what he saw. It was eclectic, kind of chaotic, and perfectly Hazel. She was going to love it.

All that was left was fetching the birthday girl, which was a job Thomas was eager to do. He couldn't wait to wrap his arms around her waist and give her a birthday kiss.

When he showed up to the house, the door was ajar. An immediate sense of dread flooded Thomas's body, freezing him to the spot. Something was wrong. He ran into the house, shouting for Hazel. The muffled voice calling to him from upstairs sent his heart into overdrive.

Thomas took the steps two at a time. He couldn't find Hazel in her room or the bathroom. He pushed open the door to the spare bedroom and stopped in his tracks, trying to make sense of the scene in front of him.

Hazel's body was wrapped in layers of gauze, with loose strands trailing on the ground. She held her hands out and walked towards him, swaying from side to side. "Sorry I'm moving slowly today. I'm almost ready."

Thomas dipped the mummified mess, kissing the tip of her nose. "How long did it take you to get ready?" he asked.

"Way longer than I thought. It worked out though." Hazel ran a hand down Thomas's cape. "I like your Zorro costume."

"Thanks." He lowered the mask to cover his eyes. "I wanted to make sure you'd recognize me in a crowd in case you get in any danger."

"I'd be able to spot you in a crowd of a hundred Zorros." The kiss Hazel gave him didn't leave much room for doubt.

"Speaking of danger, did you know your front door was open? I thought something was wrong."

Hazel smacked her forehead. "I had armloads of bandages that I carried up here. I thought I had closed it."

"Well, I'm going to count finding you safe and sound as my first act of heroism today." Thomas cupped his hand to her chin, wishing some of the bandages were moved so he could touch her face.

"How are you feeling about your party?"

Hazel blinked a few times to clear her eyes. "Is it strange to say that my heart is sad but I'm also super excited?"

"Not strange at all." Thomas held out his arm. "Let's get the birthday girl to her main event." He may not be a hero in real life, but he sure felt like one when Hazel grabbed a crown with one hand and his arm with the other. He was going to do everything in his power to make sure she had a birthday no one would forget.

CHAPTER 19

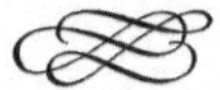

The ride to her birthday party was a little uncomfortable with the outfit she was wearing, but Hazel kept a smile on her face. Thomas seemed to love her the way she looked, mummified bandages and all. He was going to flip out when he saw what her real costume was.

He had tried so hard to make her birthday special, but Hazel's heart wasn't there. She couldn't explain to her friends how heartbreaking it was to have the person who made every day special for her no longer there. Her dad had moments of lucidity, but most of the time he forgot who he was. Hazel was stuck with a lifetime of memories and no one to share them with.

Being raised by a single dad was a statistic that textbooks liked to talk about. There certainly had been some hard moments where she wished her mom was more present. Talking to her dad about her first crush had been awkward, but she knew he'd support her no matter what.

The conversation had happened between clients at the clinic. By the time the next animal arrived for treatment, Hazel had a confidence boost to talk to the boy she thought was cute.

Her dad gave her the strength to do anything she wanted, which was why Hazel knew she'd be able to plaster a smile on her face and keep it there through her party. She was prepared to be brave, but her nerves had other plans. By the time they arrived in front of the residential care facility, Hazel was ready to go home.

"Are you doing okay?" Thomas asked.

Hazel must have been letting her smile slip. She was going to have to try harder. "Yep. I'm just really excited."

Thomas lifted his hand to her face, and she leaned into it, taking strength from her cowboy.

"We're not in any hurry," he said. He lifted her chin so she could look him in his melting eyes. "If you want to go home, I'll cover for you."

The offer was tempting. Hazel's heart was being held together by the thin gauze bandages she wore. All it would take was one wrong word, or one sideways glance from a friend, and she'd be leaving the party in tears. That wasn't any way to celebrate turning thirty.

"Can we stand here for a minute?" she asked.

Thomas nodded, pulling her close. "Take all the time you need."

The door swung open a minute later and Steph poked her head out. "What's taking you so long? Everyone is here."

Hazel's heart began to race. She wasn't ready to go

in yet.

Thomas wrapped his arm more firmly around Hazel's body, giving her shoulder a gentle squeeze. "I need a minute with my birthday girl," he told Steph. "I'll let you have her soon."

Steph rolled her eyes and went back inside, muttering something about lovebirds under her breath.

"Thanks." Hazel rested her cheek on Thomas's chest. "You definitely wore the right costume for saving me tonight."

Thomas took a step back and reached for her hands. "Hazel, I always want to be there for you. I know I'm going to say and do the wrong things at times but taking care of you is all I want to do. I'd never intentionally hurt you."

Her heart sped up. They had been dating for barely a month, but it sounded like Thomas was ready to propose. If he knelt down, she was going to flee the scene. Birthday party or not, she was definitely not ready for that sort of a conversation.

She tensed; her body coiled like a spring. She had to stop Thomas before he said something he couldn't take back.

"I know we haven't been seriously dating for very long." He plowed forward, with no indication of stopping. "But for me, it feels like eternity."

The chance to stop Thomas was slipping away. "Not yet," she whispered. Breaking up with her best friend right before a birthday party was not what she had been planning to do, but that was where the evening was heading.

Thomas stopped. "Not yet? What does that mean?"

Hazel gulped. "It sounds like you are getting ready to propose. And I'm not ready yet."

The words were out. Hazel expected her world to come crashing down when Thomas realized she wasn't on the same page as him. She turned away, looking over her shoulder, but Thomas gently lifted her chin.

His chocolate eyes were crinkled as a smirk lifted his cheek. "Wait. You thought I'd propose to you after only a few weeks of dating? I may be crazy about you, but I'm not that crazy."

"But you sounded so serious." Relief blasted through Hazel's body, lifting her spirits.

The smoldering look was back in Thomas's eyes when his hands slid down her back to rest on her waist. "I promise I am not going to propose to you any time soon. But if things keep going how they have been, I may have to eat my words."

Hazel laughed. "Alright. But just be warned that if you are going to be proposing, it better be when I'm dressed up looking beautiful. This mummy costume doesn't scream romantic."

Thomas shook his head, lifting the edge of the birthday girl sash she wore. "I disagree. You are beautiful no matter what you are wearing."

The door opened again, and Steph stepped out, planting her hands on her hips. "Are you two done kissing yet?"

A quick glance at Thomas's face gave Hazel all the courage she needed. She rolled her eyes and shook her head while Thomas shook with laughter beside her. "Yes, Steph. We're coming."

She bounded up the steps to her party, hyper aware of the man following right behind, his hand clasped in hers. It was time to put on her smile and dance the night away.

* * *

HAZEL WAS LEANING against the drink table, trying to catch her breath, when movement off to the side caught her attention. She had been keeping tabs on her dad through the party. He seemed happy, walking around to greet people as if he had never met them before. Hazel wouldn't tell him that he had been many of those people's vets for years.

She turned to see what the commotion was, but Thomas reached for her hand, pulling her attention back to him. "Keep your eyes on mine," he said. "Don't ruin Steph's surprise."

He was trying to help, but all it did was add fuel to the flame of Hazel's curiosity. Then again, being forced to stare at Thomas's face was hardly a punishment. Hazel rested her hands on his chest.

"Are you enjoying my birthday?" she asked.

"I actually am. How are you holding up?"

Hazel stopped to think about her answer instead of giving her standard brush-off. "Honestly, it's going better than I expected. I'm sad my dad doesn't recognize me, but he seems to be having a great time."

"I'm so glad. I was a little worried." Thomas ran his hand up her arm, laughing as he did so. "Please don't take this the wrong way. Your costume is fun, but I miss being able to play with your hair."

"You don't love my mummy look? Don't worry. That will be changing soon." If Hazel guessed correctly, Steph had been wheeling out a big cake. They were trying to surprise Hazel, but she was the one with the surprise planned.

"Can I get the birthday girl over here?" Steph asked. She was standing shoulder to shoulder with Millie and Dawn, hiding the table behind them.

Hazel raised her hand in the air. "That's me!" She made her way over to the women, stopping to hug a couple of friends on her way to the front of the room.

"Are you ready for your cake?" Millie asked.

Hazel shook her head. "Not yet. I have something I'd like to say." She looked at the sea of faces who had come to support her, tearing up when she saw the love that had been put into her party. Even though the decorations were falling and some of the costumes looked like they had been thrown together in five minutes, more people had shown up than she could have imagined. Senior citizens mingled with young faces, smiles present on each of them.

Hazel lowered her hand to her side, prodding her costume until she found the piece of gauze she was looking for. "Thanks to everyone who is here. I think you all know how much I like my birthdays."

That earned a few chuckles from the crowd.

"Well, these past few years have been filled with ups and downs. I grew a lot over the past decade, but I personally am ready to leave my twenties behind me."

Hazel tugged at the gauze, making the tail longer. She pressed it into Dawn's hands. "Don't let go," she whispered. She reached down and found another loose end which she handed to Steph. "You both need to hold on tight."

"Please join me while I shed my twenties and step forward into my thirties as a new person." She took off the tiara, untied the sash, and handed them to Thomas. After a quick check to make sure her friends were ready, she began to spin.

At first the crowd was silent, with a few titters breaking the quiet. But slowly, as Hazel continued to turn, they began to clap. Each rotation unwrapped a little more of the costume underneath until Hazel was standing straight, wearing a sparkling dress. She took the sash from Thomas and slipped it over her shoulder before she put the tiara back on.

Hazel cleared her throat and the crowd quieted down. "I don't know what the next decade will bring, but whatever it does, I'm so excited to have you by my side. Thank you for being my support system."

"We love you, Hazel," Dawn said. She and Millie stepped to the side, revealing a two-tiered birthday cake that looked like a Steph creation. Hay poked out from the sides, with a red barn sitting on the top. As Hazel looked closer, she realized that the animals in front of the barn were candles.

Hazel took in every detail while her friends sang to her. At the end of the song, a voice she knew piped up from the back of the room.

"That's my baby girl. It's her birthday today."

Hazel's eyes flew to the corner where her dad stood. His eyes were bright with recognition. She pushed her way through the crowd to her dad's side, throwing her arms around his neck.

"Happy birthday, sweetheart," he said. The warmth was back in his voice, like he was talking to someone he loved instead of a stranger.

Hazel wiped at the tears in her eyes, trying to hide her emotion from her dad, but he was too observant.

"What's wrong?"

The concern on his face tore her heart open. She had spent so many visits, waiting for him to remember her, and now he did.

"It's my birthday today, Daddy."

"I know, sweetheart. You're growing up too fast." A cloud passed across his face, and Hazel knew she had moments left. If he was still lucid, there was one person she wanted him to meet. She scanned the room, relieved to see Thomas walking towards her. He stopped a few feet back to give her privacy, but Hazel reached for his hand.

"Daddy. This is my friend Thomas."

"Tommy Matthews? I've known you since you were knee high."

"It's good to see you, Mr. Wright." Thomas held on to her dad's hand.

"I'm dating him, Daddy. He is the man I love." She said the words, hoping they would pierce through her dad's faulty memory, but he was already fading too fast.

"That's nice, dear. Love is good. I used to love someone." His brow wrinkled with concern while he tried to focus. "Do I know you? You remind me of someone." With that, he was locked in his mind, the recognition gone.

Hazel couldn't breathe. The pressure on her body was too strong. She gasped for air and pushed out of Thomas's arms, running for the open door and the fresh air outside. The tears didn't hit until she was halfway across the parking lot.

When Thomas caught up with her, her body was shaking. "He was there, Thomas."

"I know." He pulled Hazel close, his hands comforting as they stroked her hair. "I'm so sorry we had the party here."

Hazel glanced towards the building. "You don't understand. He was there. He came to my party and for the briefest of moments, he knew who I was. You gave me my dad today."

Thomas grunted, swiping at his eyes.

"Are you crying?" She didn't think Thomas could get any more endearing, but this was a new side of him.

"Hey. Cowboys are allowed to cry too." He twisted a strand of her hair, his hand soft against her neck. "I am so glad you're okay."

Hazel pressed her cheek to his hand. "Thank you for my birthday party. If we had gone to Cocoa Castle, I would have missed out on that moment with my dad."

Thomas straightened up, his hand still. "You knew about the restaurant?"

"Millie may have let it slip a couple of months ago. She's the worst at keeping surprises." Hazel waited until Thomas began combing his fingers through her hair before she spoke again, gathering her thoughts.

"I meant what I said." Hazel let her body relax into Thomas's comforting arms.

"About the party?" Thomas's brow furrowed. "I'm confused."

"I meant what I said to my dad about you being the man I love." She held her breath, waiting for Thomas to respond. Then she pushed back from him so she could study his liquid eyes.

"I've said it to you so many times, it feels like part of our normal conversations. But Thomas, I want you to understand me. I truly, genuinely, love you with every part of my soul. These past few weeks with you have been some of the happiest moments of my life."

There was the briefest of pauses before Thomas wrapped his arms around her, lowering his chin to kiss Hazel until there was no question in her mind that he loved her back. She was breathless when he stepped back.

"I know I've said those words hundreds of times before as well, but Hazel, you are my life and my heart. I love you too." He pressed the most tender of kisses to her lips and reached for her hand.

"Unfortunately, there's a group of people in there who will be very upset if I don't take you back. Are you ready?"

Hazel nodded. She didn't care what happened to the rest of her party. With Thomas by her side, she was exactly where her heart wanted her to be.

CHAPTER 20

$\mathcal{H}$azel stood outside her office, blowing on her hands to warm them up. October was already gone, and November was coming to a close. Somewhere along the way, the fall leaves had dropped completely, making way for a dusting of snow that lined the branches of the trees. Temperatures had plummeted, leaving each remote job a little more difficult to do.

She was heading out to a ranch she hadn't been to before. Mr. Gates was known for his gruff exterior and his reputation for refusing to accept help. If he was calling Hazel in, something had to be really wrong.

Hazel wasn't entirely sure what the problem was. All Mr. Gates said was that his horse was hurting, and he didn't know how to help it. It made packing the truck full of the right supplies a little more difficult than normal. By the time Hazel left, she was sure she was carrying far more bandages than she'd possibly need, but she was erring on the side of overpacking rather than facing a grumpy rancher to tell him why she couldn't finish the job.

She was getting ready to pull out for the job when Thomas called. It had been over a month since her birthday, and yet his name still sent flutters of excitement through her body. She loved spending time with her handsome rancher.

"Where are you off to?" Thomas asked.

"The Gates ranch." Hazel re-fastened the clamp on one of the bins that had popped open.

"Seriously? I've seen that family twice that I can remember. The first time he yelled at me for crossing the street too slowly. The second time, we were at the auction, and I outbid him on a horse. I'm pretty sure he hates my guts."

"He can't be that bad." Hazel backed out of the parking spot, watching to make sure no clients were pulling in when she drove away. "I mean, he sounded like the visit was urgent, but I don't think I need to worry for my life."

Thomas snorted. "I can come for moral support."

"And risk him shooting you for trespassing? No thank you." Hazel didn't need an angry rancher glowering over her shoulder while she worked. "Besides, I have my rusty taekwondo skills to call on if things get sketchy."

"Alright. If anyone can handle herself against an angry rancher, it's you. Call me when you're home?"

He didn't have to ask. Hazel knew she'd be dialing Thomas's number as soon as she got in her truck to give him a report. It felt nice to have a boyfriend to check in with.

* * *

By early December, Hazel had settled into a routine that included Thomas. They'd video chat in the morning over breakfast, and then she was off to the vet's office while he checked on the animals at the ranch. Their lunch breaks were usually short, but they met together as often as they could. Getting a quick hug before heading back to work gave Hazel a boost of energy to carry her through the hardest days.

They couldn't get together every evening, but Hazel made her way to the ranch whenever she could. It felt good to be included in Thomas's world, where his family treated her like one of their own.

It was during one of the family dinners that the first inkling of doubt crept in about her relationship. She had been watching Emily and Porter move together as a team. Emily would wash a dish and Porter was standing right beside her to dry it. If Emily sat on the couch, Porter was there beside her. He would play the piano and she'd hum alongside him.

Bree was the one who started the conversation. She looked at Porter and Emily, much like Hazel had been doing, and then she asked Porter when he was going to propose.

Emily buried her blushing face in her hands, but Porter met his sister's eye. "I think it's clear that I'm totally and completely in love with this woman. We are still getting to know each other though."

The love on Emily's face was evident as she looked up

at Porter. "There's a big difference between loving someone and being prepared to spend the rest of your life with them," she said. "Porter and I still have some of the big questions to talk about to make sure we're a good match long term. When I get married, I plan to make it last."

Hazel was impressed with their answer. They were going to make a beautiful couple when they finally made their vows.

"Got it," Bree said. "So, you guys are going to get married eventually?"

Porter laughed. "Why is this on your mind?" He reached over to tousle his sister's hair.

Bree crossed her arms in front of her body. "Well, if you get married, I'll get to be in the wedding, right. Winter formal gave me some ideas for bridesmaid's dresses."

That made sense to Hazel. Bree had been looking for her latest formal dance dress.

"How about this?" Emily asked. "If we do get married, I pinky promise you can be in our wedding."

Bree pumped her fist in the air, but then she turned her attention to Thomas and Hazel. "So, how about you guys? Do I get to be in your wedding too?"

Thomas choked on the water he was trying to drink. "Who says we're getting married?"

His words shot through Hazel like a lightning bolt striking a tree. They hadn't talked about marriage, but in her heart, Hazel figured that was where they were headed. Had she read the situation completely wrong? Maybe she was just a fling to Thomas.

"Well, you guys are sappy in love like Porter and Emily," Bree said.

Mom Matthews piped in. "Bree, you can't bother your siblings about getting married just so you can get a dress. There's a lot more that goes into a marriage than the actual wedding day. Pretty dresses go out of style, but marriage is eternal."

Reid pulled on Bree's ponytail. "I tell you what. When I get married, I'll let you be in my wedding."

"Thanks," Bree said, "but you're not really dating anyone. I don't want to wait years before I can dress up again." She stuck her tongue out at Reid, dodging to the side when he reached for her ponytail again.

Hazel tuned out the rest of the conversation, spiraling downwards with her thoughts. Had she and Thomas become too comfortable? They had been great friends before they started dating. Once they added kissing to the friendship, the relationship grew deeper, but had they stagnated?

She couldn't remember the last conversation where they had discussed something serious. They were so comfortable together, they had fallen into a rut.

Thomas squeezed her hand, causing her to look up. All the eyes on the table were trained on her face.

"So?" Bree asked.

Hazel shook her head slightly. "Sorry. I was lost in my thoughts. What did you say?"

"I asked if I could be in your wedding too."

It would have been easy to say yes to Bree, but Hazel's mind was spinning out of control. She glanced down at her phone as it began to ring and then pressed it to her ear. "This is Hazel," she said, excusing herself from the table.

Clients often called at the most inopportune time, but this time, she was more than grateful for the interruption. There was a cow with a broken ankle and Hazel's services were needed. She grabbed her purse from the couch and excused herself.

"Thanks," she mouthed to Mom Matthews.

Hazel's breathing didn't slow down until she was driving down the highway, away from the probing questions. There was no doubt that she had fallen hard for Thomas. Was it enough?

THREE DAYS later Hazel was still avoiding Thomas. She blamed her lack of communication on being busy with clients, but the truth was much harder to face. If she started talking to Thomas, they were going to need to have a real conversation. They couldn't keep dating each other with no plans for the future, but the thought of making plans was terrifying. They might find something that would tear them apart, and then her friend would be gone.

On the fourth day, she was caught by surprise when he came to her work. Her body was drained after working with an especially difficult patient. The cat was going to live, but she had been taking longer to wake up from the anesthesia than normal. Hazel needed a few minutes to clear her mind before her next patient.

She was scrubbing her hands when Thomas knocked

on her door. Jana knew better than to let anyone back after surgeries, but she was watching the cat while Hazel took a few minutes to relax. With no one at the front desk, it was normal for Thomas to walk back to Hazel's office.

"What are you doing here?" she asked. Her body was weary, with no strength left for a difficult conversation.

Thomas paused in the open doorway. "I was hoping we could talk. You've been avoiding me and I want to know why."

Hazel glanced up. "This really isn't a good time. I'm with a patient."

"In your office? I don't see any animals here." Thomas stepped into the room.

"I just finished surgery a little while ago. I need to . . ." She trailed off, her stomach tightening. "It doesn't matter if you can tell what I'm working on. If I say I'm with a patient, that's what I mean." He didn't have any right to judge her.

Thomas flinched. "You're right. I don't know what you are working on. I'll come back later."

He turned and walked out of the office, his boots thudding down the hall. Hazel wanted to run after him and tell him to stay, but that wouldn't help with anything. They weren't going to solve their problems during her five-minute break.

She walked to the back room where Jana was sitting with the cat. "How's our patient doing?"

"She's starting to come out of the anesthesia now. I'm sure that before long, Luna here will be hunting mice again."

"Thanks for sitting with her. I wouldn't be able to do this job without you."

Jana scratched the top of the cat's head. "Are you doing okay? You're stretched so thin these days that I worry about you. Between that handsome cowboy of yours and all the late-night emergency calls, I don't know how you are upright."

Jana's words were a gut punch.

"I'm not sure how much longer Thomas will be a distraction."

"What do you mean?" Jana gasped. "You guys aren't breaking up, are you?"

Hazel had to find the words to explain why she was struggling. "No. At least not yet. I think we jumped into dating too fast. On paper, it seems so easy to cross the line from friendship to love. In reality, we skipped a bunch of the important steps."

"I'm not following. Skipping all the awkward stuff sounds awesome. You don't have to do the song and dance of wondering if he'll actually like you once he gets to know you."

"Yeah, but we also missed all the things that would be warning signs if I was dating someone from the start. Those stupid habits that wear a person down. What if he bites his nails or talks with his mouth full of food?"

Jana raised her eyebrows, smirking at Hazel. "You already know he doesn't do those things. I'm also pretty sure you would have noticed by now if he was a chronic throat clearer or if he had any disgusting habit that would be a deal breaker."

"You're right. I guess it comes down to the more serious questions. Where would we live if we were married? Would he expect me to quit my job and raise kids if we have any? What religion do we raise the family as? How do we budget?"

Hazel was spinning out of control. Each question wrapped around her heart like a vice. She wrapped her arms around her stomach, trying to keep the panic at bay while more and more questions raced through her mind.

Jana rested a hand on her shoulder. "It sounds like these are questions you need to discuss with Thomas. Maybe then you'd be able to stop stressing out."

"You're right, but I don't know how to do that."

Jana gave her a hug. "I know the conversation will feel uncomfortable, but you guys have such a solid foundation, I think you'll be fine. It sounds harsh, but stop being a chicken. You've got this."

Hazel took a deep breath. "Thanks. And you're right. I need to face my fears instead of hiding from them."

Jana went back to work, and Hazel spent the rest of the afternoon thinking about what kind of conversation she wanted to have. By the time she locked up the clinic, she was ready to be brave. It was time to call her cowboy.

CHAPTER 21

Thomas was surprised when Hazel called. She had been so dismissive earlier at the clinic. He was even more surprised when she asked him over to her house. She didn't say why, but Thomas hoped he had been forgiven for whatever he had done.

When he got to the house, the first thing he noticed was the smell of fresh baked cookies. Hazel greeted him at the door with a quick kiss and then she ran to turn the timer off.

Thomas followed behind. "Do you need any help?" he asked, feeling like he had stepped into an alternate universe where they hadn't been fighting.

"Yeah. Can you grab two mugs?" Hazel was sliding cookies onto a cooling rack.

If Thomas didn't know better, he'd think he was on the set of a baking show, and not in his girlfriend's kitchen. The cookies were throwing him off. Last he knew, Hazel was upset with him. Most people didn't bake cookies for people they were fighting with.

Thomas placed the mugs on the counter next to the stove, where a pot of water was already simmering. "So." He leaned against the counter so he could study Hazel's face. "How did the rest of your day go?"

Hazel shook her head. "I don't want to talk about work right now." She stepped to Thomas's side and wrapped her arm around his waist.

"Okay." Thomas wasn't sure what to think. "What do you want to talk about then? Will you tell me what I did wrong?"

Hazel switched the stove off and pointed to the mugs. "Let's make our cocoa and then maybe we can talk on the couch?"

They stirred their cocoa in silence, the spoons sounding extra loud as they clinked against the side of the mugs. Thomas followed behind Hazel as she carried a plate of cookies to the coffee table, setting it down in the center.

After a minute, she started to speak. "Dinner with your family kind of freaked me out."

"I figured as much. Can you tell me why?"

Hazel took a sip of her cocoa. "Listening to Porter and Emily talk made me realize that we have fallen into a rut."

"Huh. Why do you say that?"

Hazel fixed her blue eyes on his. "Where do you see this relationship going?"

The question would be easy to deflect, but Thomas was pretty sure she wanted a real answer. "Honestly? I'd marry you tomorrow if I thought you'd let me."

That was clearly not the answer Hazel was looking for. She reached for a blanket, wrapping it around her shoulders. "How can you say that?"

"That I'd marry you? Because I've been in love with you for years. What are we waiting for?"

She shook her head. "We haven't even talked about the important questions. What if we're not as compatible as we think?"

Thomas was trying to be present, but Hazel's questions felt hostile. Facing a charging bull felt safer than trying to come up with an answer that wouldn't make her mad. "I think we're plenty compatible, but obviously you don't. Will you tell me what you want to know?"

Hazel ran a hand through her hair. "It's all the basics. The stuff that would make a difference in a long-term relationship, like where we'd live and how we'd raise children if we had any."

"You're right. What if we make a list?" Thomas asked. He reached for his mug, shaking it slightly so the marshmallows swirled in a lazy circle.

"A list?" Hazel pushed back a layer of the blankets. "What kind of a list?"

Thomas swallowed another sip of cocoa, letting the warmth give him courage in case his idea backfired. "Can we make a list of all the hard topics? The things that might make us too different?"

"What would be the good in that?" Hazel blew on her cocoa.

Thomas set his mug down on the coffee table and folded his hands in his lap. "I don't know. I mean, maybe it would do more harm than good, but if we really aren't a good match, I want to know before I fall too deeply in love with you." He pulled her close, placing a gentle kiss on her forehead. "Although, I'm already pretty smitten. I don't know if I can fall any further in love."

Hazel leaned away from his embrace. "You don't think we're a good match?"

"I didn't say that." He swirled the marshmallows in his mug once more, trying to figure out how to say what was on his heart. "Okay. Here's the thing. I think we've proven that we're physically compatible. It is no secret I enjoy kissing you, and I think you like kissing me back. Would you agree?"

Hazel's eyes shone while a shy smile crossed her face. "Maybe a little bit." She brushed her hand down his arm, sending heat blasting through his body.

"Or maybe a whole lot. I'm pretty sure if all a relationship took was kissing, we'd be in great shape."

That earned a laugh from Hazel. "Agreed."

"The way I see it, the main thing that will get me in trouble is my mouth. I don't want to do something that will push you away."

"Me either."

"Let's make a list to see how many things are really going to be in our way." Thomas shifted in his seat. He hoped she'd go with the idea.

"Won't that give us a lot of things to fight about?" Hazel's eyes were sad.

Thomas wanted to take back his words. "I hope not. It

could show us that maybe we really are on the same page about most things."

Hazel leaned over and grabbed her purse, pulling out a small notebook. "How about this? We can make a list, but we can't discuss more than one item at a time. And each item needs to be discussed over some sort of a dessert."

"I like it." Thomas sat up, folding his hands in his lap. "Since we have cookies and cocoa, does that mean we can address one issue?"

Hazel squeezed his leg. "Let's get the list made."

Thomas nodded, happy they were finding a solution. "Okay. Here we go."

He drew the numbers one and two on the paper and circled each of them. "You mentioned where we'd live and how we'd raise our kids. That's one and two. I guess number three could be how many kids we want."

Hazel tensed up beside him, not saying a thing.

"What's wrong?" The tension in the room was making it hard to breathe.

"What if I never want kids?" Hazel's words hung in the air, a dagger waiting to fall.

Thomas could feel the warning in his heart to choose his words wisely. "Is that how you really feel? That you don't ever want kids?" He spun the pen in his hands.

"I didn't say that, but I might not. Maybe my practice will be too much for me to handle. Maybe I'll wait too long to get pregnant, and I'll miss a window."

"You're worrying about hypothetical maybes?" Thomas asked. "That seems a little silly to me."

Hazel folded her arms across her chest, her eyes

narrowing. "You think the decision to have kids or not is a silly one."

"Not at all. I think that worrying about it when we have so many things going right for us is a little silly."

Hazel reached for the notebook and flipped it closed, tucking it back in her purse. "Never mind. I shouldn't have said anything." She reached for her cocoa and took a sip, acting as if nothing had happened.

"So that's it? We can't even have a discussion?" Thomas pushed against the edge of the coffee table. "I thought our friendship was deeper than that." He could feel the frustration clawing through his body. He wasn't the one who had pushed Hazel away. She was the one who had been holding back.

Hazel sat up from the couch. "I'm not really ready for this conversation," she said.

Thomas nodded. "Then I guess I have some things I need to finish at home." He walked to the kitchen and dropped his mug in the sink before leaving. "Thanks for the cocoa."

"So, we're done talking?" Hazel asked.

Thomas nodded. "There doesn't seem to be much point." He headed towards the front door, pausing in the opening to wave goodbye to Hazel. "I'm sorry it didn't work out."

"Me too." Hazel buried her face in her hands. Thomas wanted to comfort her, but he knew Hazel wouldn't appreciate it. Instead, going against every instinct in his body, he walked out the door, leaving a large part of his heart with her.

Once he got home, Thomas headed to his room and locked the door behind him. The only person he wanted to talk to had just dashed all his hopes and dreams. He knelt by his bed, choosing to talk to the person who knew both of them infinitely. If anyone had answers, it would be the Lord.

* * *

A WEEK LATER, Hazel was still avoiding Thomas. He had tried to reach out a couple of times, but he had his pride. He wasn't going to grovel when she clearly wanted nothing to do with him.

There were plenty of jobs to keep Thomas's mind distracted. With fall ending, it was time for an extra push to make sure they were prepared for the winter. The last of the hay bales had been harvested, and the barns were filled. Now all that was left were the little odds and ends that popped up.

What Thomas craved was heavy work, lifting bales or digging ditches until he was so sore, he collapsed into bed each night. If his muscles were hurting, he had less time to worry about his heart.

Thoughts of Hazel would pop up at the most inconvenient times. Thomas was clearing out a corner of the tool shed when the faint sound of meowing caught his attention. He moved aside a flowerpot to find a litter of kittens, barely a few days old.

Mable was licking them while they nursed, clearly comfortable in her new role as a mom.

"Good job, Momma," Thomas said. He knelt back to watch the kittens squirm around and his memories flew back to the visit at Hazel's vet clinic. He grunted and headed for the tools on the far side of the shed. Surely there was something somewhere that needed to be hammered.

There wasn't time for emotions. Especially when Hazel wasn't willing to work things out. Thomas wandered to the woodpile and threw his hammer to the side, picking up an axe instead. He had already chopped enough wood to last a couple winters, but it never hurt to chop more. As he swung the axe down through the wood, he pushed all thoughts of Hazel to the side. A cowboy worked. He didn't let feelings get in the way of the job.

Thomas headed over to the field to check on Hannah and her foal. The foal had been born a few weeks earlier, and she was looking strong. Thomas topped off the water trough, even though barely an inch had been drunk. Anything to keep his hands busy. He was walking across the field when he noticed his dad's horse, Sunflower, her head hanging low.

"Hi there, girl," he said, approaching her from the front. She didn't lift her head or whinny to greet him.

Concern flew through Thomas's veins like liquid ice, freezing him to the spot. There were reminders of his dad all over the ranch, but Sunflower was a special one. She was the horse his dad was riding when he met Mom Matthews. She was the first horse each of the Matthews children learned to ride on when they were growing up. Of all the animals on the ranch, she was woven the most thoroughly through all their lives.

Thomas rested his hand on Sunflower's side. Standing close, her wheezing was audible. He looked at her eyes, which were glazing over.

Suddenly, it didn't matter what Thomas thought about Hazel. His horse was sick, and she was the only one who could help. He called the clinic instead of her home phone so Jana would answer.

"Elk Mountain Veterinary Clinic. How can I help you?"

Thomas gripped the phone to his ear. "Jana. It's Thomas. I need Hazel's help."

"She's not available right now," Jana said. "Can I pass a message along?"

Thomas picked up a rock and threw it, holding back a yell. Hazel had obviously told Jana to screen her calls. "It's my dad's horse, Sunflower. She's really sick." His voice broke as he clasped the phone tightly. "Look, I know Hazel is upset with me, but she's the only one who has a chance of helping Sunflower. Please send her over. I'll have my mom meet her. She won't even have to see me."

Jana cleared her throat. "I'll see what I can do."

When she hung up, the dam of emotions that had been building up inside Thomas broke. He threw his hat to the ground and bent down, grabbing a handful of rocks which he hurled further and further, ignoring the tears that cascaded down his cheeks.

The few minutes it took for Jana to call back felt like an hour. When Thomas picked up his phone his voice was raw from shouting to the wind about all the frustrations in his life.

"She'll come by after work," Jana said.

"Thank you." Relief flooded through Thomas's body. Sunflower had a chance.

Jana's next words doused his heart. "And Thomas?"

"Yeah?"

"She doesn't want to see you."

Thomas picked up his hat and dusted it off. The time for crying about Hazel was over.

"I understand."

He hung up the phone and gave Sunflower a final pat. "Hold on, girl. Help will be here soon."

CHAPTER 22

azel's stomach dropped when Jana told her about Thomas's horse. She had been avoiding him, but making up a sick animal so she'd have to come visit was a new low for him. Why couldn't he just respect her space?

Still, as the town's only large animal vet, she couldn't exactly ignore the call. Sunflower probably had aching bones again. She was an older horse, and her arthritis flared up occasionally. Hazel knew she had to head to the Matthews family ranch, just to make sure things were okay. She had been treating Sunflower for minor injuries for years, and this would be no different.

Jana answered the clinic's phone while Hazel gathered her things to leave. She had her hand on the doorknob when Jana called for her to come back.

"I've got someone on the phone who found a dog off to the side of the street. It looks like a hit and run, but she wants to make sure the dog is okay. Can you stay for an assessment, or should I send her to the after-hours clinic?"

A mixture of trepidation and relief chased through Hazel's body. The injuries could be bad for the dog, but at least she had an excuse to stay at the clinic longer before facing Thomas.

"They can come here." She headed back to her office to pull on her lab coat. The fake injury at Thomas's house would have to wait while Hazel dealt with a real animal in distress.

Jana was drumming her fingers on the desk when Hazel came out.

"I didn't ask if you were okay staying late," Hazel asked. "Can you help me?"

Jana pulled her hair back into a ponytail. "Of course. But it's not me I'm worried about. It's you and Thomas. Don't you need to head to his ranch to help with Sunflower?"

Hazel shook her head. "It's not a real emergency. Thomas just wants to talk to me."

"How do you know?" Jana picked at her fingernail polish. "He sounded pretty upset."

That threw Hazel for a moment, but she ignored the nagging voice at the back of her head whispering that maybe she should call Thomas just to check in. "I've been avoiding him. I think he is trying to find an excuse to make me visit."

The look on Jana's face said she clearly didn't agree, but Hazel was already committed to the patient coming in. She couldn't exactly tell the woman to let the dog die after all.

Even if Sunflower was sick, it wasn't going to be anything other than a simple cold.

A frantic woman arrived a few minutes later, holding a dog wrapped in a blanket. She wiped at streaks of mascara running down her cheeks. "I don't understand how someone hits a dog and doesn't even stop to see if they are okay." She began pacing in front of the desk. "Do you think you can help him?"

Jana ushered the woman into an exam room so Hazel could begin her assessment of the dog. He had a large gash down his side and the leg was clearly broken. "This guy is lucky you found him when you did. We need to get him into surgery right away."

The injuries were severe, but Hazel calmed her mind, pushing out all other thoughts. She had an operation to perform, and she couldn't let herself think about Thomas again until it was over.

As the smell of antiseptic filled the air, Hazel settled into a rhythm. Jana assisted, handing Hazel instruments and checking vitals. The operation took longer than Hazel expected but the dog was a trooper. He was placed in a small kennel to recover; his breathing steady before Hazel could relax. That was when she noticed the time.

The sun had set completely, with only the faintest sliver of a moon peeking out above the mountains. All Hazel wanted to do was go home and sleep, but she had one more stop to make. She had to visit the Matthews ranch to see Sunflower even though Thomas was most likely exaggerating her symptoms. Hazel knew she wouldn't be able to sleep until she checked all her responsibilities off her list.

As promised, Mrs. Matthews was waiting for her outside the front door. Hazel felt a pang of guilt when she noticed how she slumped against the frame. In being mad at Thomas, Hazel had inadvertently made his mom wait, potentially for hours.

"I'm sorry it took so long," Hazel said.

"I'm sure you were busy helping other patients. Thank you for coming." Mrs. Matthews led the way towards a large barn off to the side of the house.

"Can you fill me in on what's happening?" Hazel asked. She could feel the pit in her stomach growing with each step they took as Mrs. Matthews described Sunflower's symptoms. The Matthews brothers exaggerated on occasion to tease, but their mom never did. Mrs. Matthews was really concerned, which meant that Sunflower was pretty sick.

Hazel followed Mrs. Matthews into the barn. She could hear Sunflower's labored breathing before she reached the stall. That wasn't a good sign at all.

When she reached the stall, Sunflower didn't lift her head to whinny or smell Hazel's hand. Not only was she sick, but she was probably the sickest horse Hazel had seen in a long time.

Hazel's hands were shaking when she gently examined Sunflower's body. Thomas had asked for help, and she had been too stubborn to see that he actually needed it. In letting her pride take over, had she waited too long?

The important questions that Hazel had wanted answered paled in comparison to the guilt she'd feel if Sunflower died.

"Where's Thomas?" Hazel asked.

Mrs. Matthews was quiet for a moment. "He said he was respecting your space."

That made perfect sense. Thomas would have had to ask his mom to step in, taking over a job he usually did because of a promise he made to Hazel.

Mrs. Matthews didn't pry, but Hazel assumed she'd be curious as to why Thomas and Hazel weren't talking.

"You must think I'm a monster," Hazel said.

"I've found that it's not really my place to judge at all," Mrs. Matthews said. "I do know that whatever is going on between you two has Thomas feeling low. All he said was that he messed up."

That was news to Hazel. She was the one who had brought up the problem. Not him. Hazel needed wisdom from an outsider's perspective. "How did you know when you were ready to marry Mr. Matthews?" she blurted out.

Mrs. Matthews stood by the stall door, looking every bit like she belonged on the ranch even though time was starting to show in her graying hair and wrinkles. "Preston and I had a whirlwind romance. He met my roommate Amy first. The day of their date, Amy was running behind. I offered to talk to him while she was getting ready. They ended up going out that night, but I couldn't stop thinking about him."

Hazel held her stethoscope against Sunflower's chest, the rattle sounding much louder in her lungs. She listened to the other side of her lungs and the rattling was worse.

"So, what did you do?" She checked Sunflower's vitals, noting her racing heart.

Mrs. Matthews was lost in her memories. "He took Amy out that night. I was dressed in my pajamas, with my hair in pink foam curlers when she got home and told me that Preston would like to talk to me."

Hazel could imagine how mortifying it would be to have someone ask her out like that. "Did you talk to him?"

Mrs. Matthews grinned. "I wasn't going to see him, even though I was dying with curiosity. I told Amy to pass along my phone number and he could call me if he had something he needed to discuss. At the time, I genuinely thought he had questions about Amy."

"I'm guessing he didn't." Hazel pulled out a syringe and a couple of glass vials. She was enjoying the story, but she had a job to do.

"I'd like to do some bloodwork on Sunflower. She clearly has some sort of an infection. Can you help me?"

Mrs. Matthews held the harness while Hazel gathered the sample. Sunflower was so lethargic, she didn't even flinch when the needle went in.

"We went out the following night." Mrs. Matthews patted Sunflower's side. "I had no way of knowing how quickly we'd fall in love."

"When did you get engaged?" Hazel couldn't remember the exact number of years Mr. and Mrs. Matthews had been married, but it was longer than she had been alive. Obviously, they had done something right to stay together for so long.

"He proposed on our third date, and I accepted on the fourth. We were married after only knowing each other for three months."

"That's unbelievable. Most people date for a lot longer than that these days."

Mrs. Matthews smiled. "Even back then, most people thought we were moving way too fast, but I knew what my heart wanted. So did he."

"It sounds like a perfect match." Hazel had known Thomas much longer than three months. She had known him almost a half of her life. If she wasn't sure how she felt about marrying him at this point, she was probably dating the wrong guy.

"He was the perfect man for me, but we definitely had our shares of growing pains. So many of our early fights were about things that didn't really matter."

Hazel tucked her instruments back into her bag. "You must have agreed on the big issues though. Otherwise, you wouldn't have lasted so long."

"We had a lot of differences. We came from very different upbringings. In the beginning, we clashed about some big issues. Over time, we decided that the relationship we had was much more important than always being right."

"Yeah, but some things you can't and shouldn't compromise on." She slung her bag over her shoulder.

Mrs. Matthews held open the door for Hazel. "The thing I found was that over the years, a lot of the big issues really turned out to be small ones. For example, our political votes canceled each other out until the day we died, but we still voted in every election. And we still loved each other no matter which side won."

"What about family size? Did you both know you

wanted a large family?" Hazel couldn't imagine the couple wanting anything less.

Mrs. Matthews watched Hazel with an intensity that made Hazel squirm. Hazel had tried to be subtle in her questioning, but she had obviously failed.

"You would think we'd be on the same page about kids because we have so many, but that is something we had to work out. We both had ideas about our family size. I knew I wanted to be a mom. I had no idea how I'd handle pregnancy though, or how difficult it would be to raise a family. He initially only wanted two kids. A boy and a girl. It worked out in the end though."

Mrs. Matthews dusted her hands off on her jeans. "Can I offer you a bit of unsolicited advice?"

They had reached Hazel's truck. Hazel dropped her vet kit in the back of the cab and turned to face her. "Yes, please."

"I've known you for a long time now, and I know my son better. Thomas has never been happier than he has been these past couple of months while he's been dating you. I don't know where your relationship will take you, but if it leads towards something more serious, don't forget to include the Lord in your decisions. He will let you know if you guys are on the right path together."

"Thanks," Hazel said. She had been so caught up in her own mind, she had forgotten to ask the Lord where her relationship should go.

When Hazel got home, she headed for the shower. She leaned her head forward, letting the water cascade down against her neck. As she did so, she began to pray. By the time she was finished with her shower, her fingers were wrinkled like raisins, but her heart was open. She was ready to talk to Thomas. This time she'd listen to what he had to say.

* * *

THOMAS WAS WAITING outside the barn when Hazel arrived the following morning. Hazel turned off the engine, her heart fluttering at the sight of him. Even though they were fighting, his handsome face sent a wave of longing through her. She knew where her heart belonged.

Hazel grabbed the box that was sitting next to her in the truck, knowing that Thomas would be excited by the contents. She closed the flap securely so the chocolate frosted donuts wouldn't get dusty when they walked to the barn. Looking at the expression on his face, she set the box back down. There would be time for treats later, after they talked.

"How is Sunflower today?" she asked.

"Not good," Thomas said. "My mom said you came late last night."

His words stabbed Hazel in the heart. Even though Thomas wasn't accusing her of anything directly, the judgment was implied. Hazel had let him down.

"I brought an antibiotic that I think will help her today." She followed Thomas to the barn, achingly aware of the gap between them. She missed the warmth of his arm around her shoulders, making her feel like she could accomplish anything in the world. Instead, he was treating her with more formality than her regular clients.

Sunflower was laying down in her stall. Like the evening before, she didn't greet Hazel with any sort of interest. Hazel tried to push her guilt away. Being a vet was all about judgment calls, and yesterday she had chosen the animal she thought was in the most immediate danger. The dog was healing well, but no owner had stepped forward yet.

Hazel gave Sunflower an injection of strong antibiotics, praying fervently that the horse would react favorably.

"When will we see results?" Thomas asked.

"If she responds how I hope she does, she should start to feel better within twenty-four hours."

Hazel listened to Sunflower's heart and checked her other vitals. They didn't seem to be worse than when she checked her the previous night, but there wasn't any improvement either. Hazel knew she'd be swinging by after work to check on Sunflower again. She wanted to fix things with Thomas, so their next visit went more smoothly.

"Can we talk?" she asked once her instruments were tucked into her bag.

Thomas folded his arms across his chest. "I tried to talk to you before. You shut me down and then you ignored me for almost a week. In fact, I'm pretty sure if Sunflower wasn't sick, you'd still be ignoring me." His eyes were fire, and his words cut through Hazel deeper than any knife. He was right on all his accusations.

"You are probably right," Hazel said. "I don't think I'd

have called you yet. I got some clarity though, and I'd like to share that with you."

Thomas turned his back to her. "I've got animals to check."

He walked away, and Hazel's heart sank. Fixing the damage she had done was going to take more than a box of doughnuts. She hoped she could find a way to make things right before her friendship was gone forever.

CHAPTER 23

Thomas was used to solving the problems that came up on the ranch by himself. He didn't ask for help lightly, so calling Hazel to check on Sunflower hadn't been easy for him. He knew she'd be reluctant to come, but he didn't think she'd ignore him for so many hours. Thankfully, Sunflower started to perk up after the antibiotics kicked in. If she had died, Thomas didn't know what he'd do.

He was throwing chicken feed to the chickens crowding around his feet when his phone buzzed. Hazel had been trying to call him for the past few days, but it was his turn to ignore her. It seemed petty, but Thomas didn't have it in his heart to deal with fickle friends.

She had warned him that if they started dating and something went wrong, they could lose the friendship. The idea had seemed preposterous at the time, but now Thomas could see the wisdom of her words. Was this the fight that would destroy a friendship that had survived so much tragedy already?

Thomas almost answered the phone, but he didn't know what he'd say. Hazel was frustrated that they weren't talking about real things, but then when he tried to talk to her, she shut him out. How was that supposed to lead to a good relationship? He needed to clear his mind.

Thomas saddled Kellen and mounted, guiding Kellen down the road until he came to a well-worn path. Then he urged Kellen into a gallop. The wind whipped through his hair while they ran, making his eyes water. He let the emotions go and whooped as adrenaline surged through his body.

They had reached the other side of the ranch before Thomas pulled Kellen to a stop. He dismounted and walked towards a grove of trees that edged the property line. As a child, Thomas played hide and seek with his brothers while their dad worked. He loved the carefree feeling of running, not caring where he was on the ranch or who found him.

He walked to one of the trees and leaned his shoulder against the rough bark, trying to get his emotions back under control. Thomas was teetering on the brink with his relationship. He could continue to ignore Hazel's messages, or he could call her back. He sighed and closed his eyes, turning his phone over in his hands. As much as he wanted to be, he wasn't ready to talk.

He slipped the phone back into his pocket and turned to face Kellen.

"It's best if I just stick with horses." Thomas grabbed the

saddle about to swing himself back up when his phone started ringing again. Kellen snorted and turned to look at Thomas as if urging him to hurry up and answer the phone so they could get back to their ride. Thomas pulled his phone back out of his pocket.

He stared at Hazel's name, lit up on the screen. Kellen whinnied and lowered his face to nuzzle Thomas. Distracted by the horse, Thomas stumbled forward. As he caught himself, his thumb slid sideways on the phone, answering it without meaning to.

"Hello?" Hazel asked after a brief pause.

The weight in Thomas's stomach intensified. He wasn't ready to talk, but apparently the universe had other plans. "Thanks, Kellen," he muttered.

"What's that?" Hazel asked.

"It's nothing," Thomas said. He glared at his horse, but Kellen didn't seem bothered. "What do you need?"

Hazel was quiet, except for an occasional sniffle. "I messed up," she finally said. "I think if there was a handbook for how to destroy a perfectly good friendship, I found the best way to do that. I want to talk, but can we please do it face to face?"

Thomas closed his eyes and leaned against Kellen for support. He was at the crossroads again. One way would lead to him having grace for Hazel, putting them on a rocky road back to some semblance of a friendship. The other would lead to him losing that friendship for good. He knew without a doubt which scenario he'd pick.

"When do you get off work?" he asked.

"Work doesn't matter today," Hazel said. "I'd rather talk things through with you."

Thomas looked at the angle of the sun. The harsh rays were beaming in his face, which meant they only had a couple hours of daylight left.

"I can meet you in an hour. My house or yours?"

Hazel cleared her throat. "I was hoping we could meet somewhere neutral. Maybe someplace we could get a treat?"

Hope blossomed in his heart. "Ice cream or cocoa?" he asked.

"Ice cream sundaes, for sure. Is the Spotted Cow Diner okay?"

"That works. I'll see you soon."

Thomas climbed on Kellen and turned towards home. He had a date to get ready for. All he had to do was trust that the Lord would help guide the conversation.

HAZEL LOOKED beautiful with her hair pulled back. Thomas was sitting across the booth from her, but he ached to close the distance between them. Falling in love was supposed to be magical, but sitting with Hazel, it felt like he was at a job interview. The uncomfortable silence between them was full of words that needed to be said, but neither one was taking the initiative.

With the silence stretching on between them, Thomas wanted to leave. What was the point of a relationship if they couldn't even make it past ordering drinks? He closed his eyes, sending a fervent prayer to the heavens.

When he opened his eyes, Hazel was studying his face. "Thomas, how did we get here? I thought things were going well, but now there is a heavy brick pressing down on my heart whenever I think about talking to you."

Words swirled through his mind, but Thomas wasn't sure what to say. "I don't know. I feel like you pulled back on the relationship. Not me. Everything changed after we had dinner at my house."

Hazel nodded. "I got scared."

"I know." Thomas reached for the saltshaker on the table so he would have something in his hands. "I mean, I know you got scared, but can you tell me why? No matter how I look at things, my life is better with you in it. It seemed so easy for you to walk away."

Hazel nodded, tears welling in her eyes. "I wanted answers. I think I was so worried that we would hurt each other, I made it happen. I didn't let you answer any of my questions because I was afraid that if we found a reason to break up, it would destroy me."

"And so you walked away." Thomas slid the saltshaker back and forth between his hands. He was trying to listen, but frustration was clawing through his chest. "When things got remotely hard, you shut me down and treated me like garbage. That's not a relationship I can live with."

"Me either," Hazel said.

"So what do we do?"

Hazel pulled a small box out of her purse and slid it across the table. "This won't fix everything, but it is a start."

Thomas held the box, turning it over in his hands. A present was a nice gesture, but he wanted more than a simple gift.

"You can open it," Hazel said.

Thomas pulled off the blue checkered paper and wadded it in a ball that he pushed to the side of his plate. He lifted the lid and found a small spiral notebook nestled inside.

"Um, thanks?" He wasn't sure what to say. The cover had a photo of small puppies sitting in a basket on it. "Did you mean to give this to me?"

Hazel took the notebook from his hands and flipped it open to the first page. Then she handed him a pen. "Last time we tried this, I ran. I wanted to give you my running shoes as a gift like that girl did in the movie, but I didn't think you'd appreciate them. And, well, I don't like to run."

A smile tugged at Thomas's mouth. He studied the page in front of him. There were already two points written down, with a large question mark by the number three. Thomas could feel the sweat beading across his brow. He was having flashbacks to their earlier fight.

"I'm not sure this is a good idea," he said.

Hazel pulled out her own pen. "I filled in the things we had already talked about. At least the first two. I was hoping, since we are having a treat together, we could talk about the third thing."

The muscles in Thomas's stomach tightened. This entire conversation was beginning to feel a little like deja vu, and he didn't like the direction it was going. "You want to talk about how many kids we'd have?"

Hazel clasped her hands together in front of her. "The last time you brought it up, I handled it poorly. I'd like to hear your answer this time."

Thomas leaned back in his chair. The entire conversation felt like a trap, but Hazel's eyes were sincere. "I hadn't given it a lot of thought before we talked about it, but now I have. I've also given it a lot of prayer. My answer is that I want at least a couple of children. I was raised with more siblings than most. At times, that was incredibly annoying. Having them around also helped shape me into the person I am today. I want any children I have in the future to have at least one sibling to commiserate with when I drive them crazy."

Hazel nodded, her eyes never leaving his face. Thomas waited for her expression to change; for the cold to seep into her features. Instead, she pulled the notebook across the table so it was in front of her.

"Thank you for sharing that. I agree. I still don't know when I want to start a family, but I know that when I do, I don't want our child to grow up alone." She wrote the number three down and added a sentence.

"What did you write?" Thomas asked.

"Number three. How many kids do you want?" She glanced at his face. "I know that is something we'll have to figure out together if we get married, but it is something I feel like we can discuss as a team instead of me yelling at you."

Thomas held his hand out. When Hazel slid the notebook to him, he pushed it to the side and took her hand in his. "I'd like that. What else do you want to talk about?"

By the time the ice cream came, they had filled three pages of notes, covering every topic they could think of, from which side of the bed they'd sleep on to who would wash the dishes after a meal.

They were throwing out ideas when the waitress walked by. "You guys are adorable together. I couldn't help but overhear a little bit of your conversation. Are you guys engaged?"

Thomas glanced at Hazel's hand, which clearly had no ring. "Not yet," he said. As he spoke the words, he knew he'd like to change that answer before too long. He passed the waitress his credit card, ready to leave the diner.

When the bill was paid, Thomas pushed his chair back and reached for Hazel's hand. She gave it a gentle squeeze as they headed towards the door. "Anything else for our list?"

Thomas pulled her into the parking lot and shook his head. "I can't think of anything right now, but I think we've got a lot of good things to discuss."

"Me too."

"And I can't propose to you until we've talked about every single item on these three pages?" He rubbed his hand down her back before tangling his fingers in her hair.

"Nope." Hazel turned to face him, her eyes bright with desire.

Thomas pressed a light kiss to her upturned face. "And if we disagree on something?"

Hazel cupped her hand around his cheek, sending heat blasting through his body with the simple touch. "I'm pretty sure we're going to disagree on a few things."

"Then what are we going to do?" It was getting difficult for Thomas to focus on coherent sentences with Hazel finally in his arms. It had been horrible when they were fighting.

Hazel leaned back in his arms. "I think the secret is that we can disagree, as long as we can find common ground somewhere. If our common ground is a commitment to the relationship and to each other, we should be able to find our way through any situation."

"I'm going to say the wrong thing," Thomas said.

"And I'm going to freak out on occasion and handle things badly."

He pulled Hazel close and leaned his cheek against her head. "I wish I could promise you that I'd always be understanding, but I can't. It really hurt when you shut me out."

Hazel rested her hand on his chest, right over his heart. "I know. I feel bad for how I treated you. I spent so much time worrying about how things would feel if they went wrong, that I fulfilled my own fears. I hated being in our fight."

Thomas kissed the top of her head. "Let's get through this notebook, and see where life leads. No more second guessing."

"Agreed."

The kiss they shared in the parking lot was filled with hope. Thomas knew some of the subjects on the list were going to take a lot more than a simple conversation, but he was excited to get started. He couldn't wait to put a ring on Hazel's finger.

CHAPTER 24

Wrapped in sweaters, Thomas and Hazel walked hand in hand down the street. Winter had finally given way to spring, which meant that the final piles of snow were melting away, being replaced by flowering blossoms.

Thomas loved the flush of pink on Hazel's face. He stopped walking and spun her to face him, giving her a gentle kiss before they kept going. He was certainly the luckiest man he knew, and it was all because of the beautiful woman by his side.

They were heading to the Spotted Cow Diner for brownie sundaes, but there was something Thomas was looking forward to more than the delicious desserts. He waited for the hostess to seat them at a table before he pulled out the small notebook from his pocket.

The edges were rough and a little bent from being carried around all winter, but the pages had been filled in.

Thomas set the book down on the table in front of Hazel and flipped it open.

"Are you ready for our final question?" he asked.

Hazel picked up the notebook and held it against her chest. "I can't believe we're at the end. How did we do that?"

Thomas pressed a hand to his stomach. "Lots and lots of ice cream."

"I wasn't sure we'd be able to work through some of these questions. I also can't believe that the last one we're answering is the first question in the book."

The last question was the one that made Thomas the happiest. He pressed his pen to the words, even though he had read them so many times, he could recite the list in his sleep. "Where will we live once we are married?"

Hazel bit the side of her cheek. "This should be the easiest of the questions to answer, but I honestly don't know what the answer is. I don't want you to have to leave the ranch, because I know how much your family needs you."

"You're right. The family does need me. Our house isn't exactly set up for a newlywed couple, but I had an idea."

He had spent hours going over plans with Porter the day before. They had sketched out a rough outline of a house on a piece of paper, but Thomas felt shy pulling it out.

"What's this?" Hazel asked.

"Do you know the small barn at the edge of the property? We pass it whenever we go to our picnic spot."

Hazel nodded.

Thomas unfolded the paper. "I was thinking if we got married, I could convert the barn into a house of our own. If we measured right, we could fit two bedrooms in there, along with a kitchen and bathroom. What do you think?"

His proposition was met with silence while Hazel studied the plans. When she looked up, she was grinning. "I love everything about this, but there's one problem."

"What's that?" Thomas asked.

"I don't think I can wait that long for us to get married. Building a house takes forever."

Thomas cleared his throat. "We may have already started working on it," he said.

"You what?" Hazel covered her mouth. "How did you know I'd say yes?"

Her mock surprise was endearing.

"I didn't, but I hoped you'd like it. If you didn't, we figured Reid or Hudson would be able to use the house when they got married."

Hazel leaned across the table, and Thomas met her halfway with a kiss to celebrate the end of their discussions. Some of the topics had been extremely difficult to talk about. A couple of the topics required more than one discussion. In the end, Thomas had built a powerful foundation with Hazel. He didn't have a ring yet, but he knew when he did, he'd be ready to commit to eternity.

* * *

THOMAS WAS BRUSHING Kellen when Porter came to find him. "What are you up to this weekend?" he asked.

"Not much," Thomas said. "What did you need?"

Porter slid his hands into his back pockets, leaning against the stall. "Do you and Hazel want to go see the tulips with Emily and me? Emily has been asking when we could go back. I thought a picnic could be fun."

The tulip fields were in full bloom, and thanks to the Landon family, the Matthews family had secret access to Mrs. Landon's special field. Hazel was going to be delighted.

"I'll check with Hazel on timing, but we're in." He turned his attention back to Kellen, but as he did, his thoughts began to churn.

Ever since he had finished the list with Hazel at the diner, Thomas had been trying to think of the perfect place to propose. There were dozens of beautiful places around town, but none of them seemed right. The tulip fields would be ideal.

By the time the weekend arrived, Thomas was a bundle of nerves. He slid the ring box into his pocket and put on the shirt he knew Hazel liked best. There was only one chance to make the proposal perfect, and Thomas wasn't going to mess that up by looking scruffy.

The road along the tulip-lined street was packed with cars. Thomas was able to squeeze the truck into a gap between two cars, but it was a tight fit. He turned off the engine and leaned over to give Hazel a quick kiss.

"Are you sure you want to see the tulips today?" she asked. "I'm pretty sure half the town is here."

"It isn't a problem. We have our own personal spot," Thomas said. He slid out of the cab, discretely patting his pocket to make sure the box was still there. He pulled a picnic basket out of the back of the truck, handing a checkered blanket to Hazel.

Porter and Emily crossed the road in front of them, heading straight for the bush that hid the secret entrance. Porter had a cooler of drinks, the handle draped over his arm.

Thomas looked from side to side to make sure no one was following them. Then he pulled Hazel behind the bush and held open a small gate.

Emily reached out to give Hazel a hug. "Is this your first time sneaking back here? I thought we were going to be in trouble the first time Porter brought me here."

Hazel held her hand behind her, and Thomas wasted no time in grabbing it. "I've heard about this field for years, but it is one of those rumors that gets stretched more and more out of proportion every time I hear it. I think the last person I talked to said that the tulips stretched for miles and miles, rivaling the tulip fields in Holland."

Thomas gave her hand a squeeze. "Some people have very active imaginations."

"It doesn't stretch for miles, but it is still gorgeous to see," Emily said. "I'm glad we could come here together."

"Are you ladies ready?" Porter asked. He held his hand out for Emily.

Thomas was happy watching them interact. Emily was perfect for his brother. So perfect, in fact, that it was a wonder Porter hadn't proposed yet. A thought pressed into Thomas's mind, but he pushed it away, swallowing to clear a lump in his throat. There was no way that both brothers were planning to propose on the same day in the same spot.

Hazel gave his hand a little squeeze. "Are you in there?"

"Sorry. I got distracted." Thomas's mind was racing. He looked at Hazel and decided that it didn't matter what Porter planned to do. By the end of the picnic, Thomas was going to be officially engaged to Hazel.

When they got to the fallen tree that covered the path, Emily began to laugh. "Do you remember making me close my eyes so the surprise wouldn't be ruined?"

Porter stroked her arm. "It was worth it, right?"

She leaned in close. "Absolutely, even though I was scared at the time." She turned to Hazel and Thomas. "So, are you going to make Hazel close her eyes too?"

Thomas raised his eyebrows. "Is that a thing? We've already got that awful tradition with the belt. I don't think we need to add another tradition to our list."

Hazel shook her head. "I don't see what closing my eyes has to do with anything."

"I wanted Emily to be able to see all the fields at once instead of bit by bit," Porter said.

"Does it actually make a difference?" Hazel asked. "If so, I'd like to see the fields the best way possible."

Thomas grunted and passed the picnic basket to Porter before he knelt down. "You've got it, Hazel. Hop on my back. You can close your eyes and I'll carry you there."

Happiness radiated through Thomas's body when Hazel wrapped her arms around his shoulders and leaned close to whisper in his ear. "I figure we can humor them."

Thomas stood, supporting Hazel's body while he

carried her along the rest of the path. The sun beat against the side of his face, warming him from the outside. If all went well, he'd be holding hands with his fiancé on the walk back.

As they turned the final corner of the path, Emily and Porter walked ahead to set up the picnic. Thomas stopped, letting Hazel slide down off his back. "Are you ready to be amazed?" he asked.

Hazel nodded.

Thomas caressed the side of her face, kissing her lips softly before stepping to the side. "Alright. You can open your eyes."

The squeal that Hazel gave was adorable. So was her little jump up and down before she reached for Thomas's arm. "I don't know what to say."

"Do you like it?" Thomas asked.

"It's beautiful." Hazel wrapped her arms around Thomas's waist and leaned her cheek against his chest.

Thomas was rubbing Hazel's back when he caught sight of his brother kneeling on one knee in front of Emily. "Seriously?" Thomas asked as Emily's hands flew to her mouth.

Hazel looked up; her eyes concerned. "What's wrong?"

"It's nothing. It's just that my brother always has to be first."

At the mention of a brother, Hazel started to turn towards Porter. Thomas grabbed her shoulder, keeping her from turning entirely around. He took a deep breath and slid his hands down her arms until he was holding both of Hazel's hands. Then he dropped to one knee.

"Hazel, I've loved you for almost as long as I can remember. You make me a better person. You make me kinder, and you give me the strength to believe in myself. I know what my world feels like without you in it. Without you, I am a fraction of the man I can be."

He paused, letting Hazel wipe the tears from her eyes.

"Will you make me the happiest man on the earth and marry me?"

Hazel pulled him to his feet, nodding her head. "Yes."

Thomas didn't give her time to answer anything else. He wrapped his arms around her, dipping her head close to the ground while he kissed her. When he straightened up, he could hear Porter and Emily cheering.

"I forgot they were there," Hazel said.

"I didn't." Thomas glanced at his brother, who was holding Emily's hand high in the air. Porter pointed to the ring and then pumped his fist. Thomas gave him a thumbs up and then turned to Hazel. In his hurry to propose before Porter did, he had forgotten the most important thing.

"I hope you'll still marry me when you realize that I botched the proposal." Thomas reached into his pocket and pulled out the ring box.

Hazel's eyes were brimming with tears when she opened the box. Nestled between the satin fabric was a simple gold band.

"I want you to pick out the ring you love, but until you do, I thought you'd like something simpler that you can wear at work. Will you still marry me even though I forgot to pull out the ring?"

Hazel planted her hands on her hips. "We didn't cover a botched proposal in our notebook. I'll have to think about it."

Laughing, Hazel wrapped her hands around Thomas's neck. The kiss she gave him left no doubt as to what her answer would be.

Every part of Thomas's heart was complete when he reached for Hazel's hand. "I guess Bree is going to get her bridesmaid dresses after all. Are you ready to share our news?"

Hazel gave his hand a squeeze. "I can't wait."

THANKS FOR JOINING me on Thomas and Hazel's adventures. They will continue to make appearances through the Elk Mountain Series as their relationship grows. The family saga continues in A Passing Grade for the Cowboy.